Metropolis: Tales From a Small Town

METROPOLIS

TALES FROM A SMALL TOWN

Dan Salerno

DS Press

Cover art by Roger Heldt
Book design by Anne Parker

ISBN:979-8-9857725-2-4 (print)
ISBN: 979-8-9857725-3-1 (e-book)

Table of Contents

Preface. i

Mitchell Gets Pink-slipped. 1

Emmie Gets the Mail. 11

Aunt Millie and Uncle George 22

Addie Mae and Emma. 31

A Farm Family 43

Button Hole School 56

Little Mickey Grows Up 66

The Barbershop 80

Artie Gets the Scoop 91

Conversations in Farley's Cafeteria 101

Whitey Farris Opens Up. 110

Life Beyond Big Jim's 122

Friends at a Funeral 135

Saint Rose of Lima to the Rescue 148

Evie McDonald and The Luck of the Irish 162

The Gazebo. 174

Preface

The setting for this collection of stories is Metropolis — an actual town in southern Illinois. But this is not a historical book. It's a work of fiction, written with love.

My mom's family grew up in Metropolis.

She loved living there and had a childhood full of happy memories.

So, while this book mentions places that do exist in Metropolis, they are templates that serve a larger purpose — of lifting up small towns, everywhere.

Towns that could use a break. Towns that are struggling. Towns that represent the best in all of us.

Towns where hope and love still exist.

At its heart, that is what this book is all about.

Mitchell Gets Pink-slipped

Mitchell's stride was purposeful. Determined.

He was a man on a mission as he walked across the Metropolis Bridge.

The railroad bridge was built in 1914, running across the 700-foot span of the Ohio River a few miles west of the town.

But Mitchell wasn't much interested in the history of the structure.

He got to the middle, slowed to a halt and looked down. The current was swift, with spring run-off. Other than the sound of the water moving and the birds chirping nearby, it was peaceful.

When he was a kid, Mitchell used to go across the bridge on a dare with his high school buddies. Freight trains frequently went across it, albeit at a pace that was slow, but still leaving the excitement of not knowing when a train would be coming.

It was quite an adrenaline rush to counteract the teenage boredom of life in a small town.

But now, two decades later, it was the exact opposite that had drawn him here.

His life was in ruins. Divorced a year ago. A child who had died the year prior to that. And now the termination notice from his employer. With the pinkslip in his pocket, he had come to the bridge directly from work.

He pulled it out and began to read it again. "Our management team regrets to inform you, that due to developments within our industry, we will be closing our facility in Metropolis at the end of the month..."

Someone from Human Resources had explained, "Don't take it personally. It's strictly a business decision."

The 34-year-old was furious. *Not personal? How else am I supposed to take it?*

He had been hired right out of high school, putting 16 years of his life into the Good Luck Glove Company. Until recently, Mitchell's experience at the factory had been exemplary. He enjoyed the camaraderie of the co-workers. He had been promoted up to a supervisory level. In fact, the Good Luck Glove Company had once been one of the top producers of gloves worldwide. Many of its employees lived within walking distance of its Metropolis location on Market Street. Being locally owned had its advantages, like gifts of hams and jellies on holidays But, in the late 1970s, the parent company was sold to foreign investors as global competition began eating away at its customer base.

Although there were forces outside of Metropolis that controlled the destiny of the Good Luck Glove Company, Mitchell took it like a hit to the stomach. By the end of the workday, his anger had turned to an emotional numbness that was too hard to swallow.

This is it. Mitchell thought. *This is the end of the road, I should have seen this coming*, he thought.

He knew that production had been down for a few years. And the changing of ownership hadn't been a good sign. The past year or so lunchroom rumors hadn't been positive. *But that's just speculation*, he thought. *I'm not getting involved in office politics.*

Mitchell pulled out his pink slip and took one last look. Then he slowly tore it into shreds and watched them float into the Ohio River.

He began to pull one leg on top of the iron railing.

"Mitchell?" Betty Cartwright's voice was soft, even comforting. She had worked with him for a dozen years at the factory.

He took his foot down and turned to face her. "What are you doing here?"

"I followed you from work when you avoided me at lunch. And when you didn't answer me when we were punching out. I asked you if you wanted to have supper at Farley's Cafeteria."

"Must have been distracted," he said shrugging his shoulders.

"Distracted?"

"Yeah."

She sighed and pointed at the river below them. "This is something more than distracted."

They had known each other, as co-workers, for 12 years. Betty was also a supervisor, but on another line, in a different part of the building. She had watched from the sidelines when Mitchell lost his son. It had been a car accident. Two vehicles hit each other at a slippery intersection just outside of town on state highway 45. Normally snow didn't stick to the ground for long in Southern Illinois, but the conditions turned to freezing rain. Drivers weren't used to it, so the Massac County Sheriff's Department was kept busy that morning. Mitchell's wife had been bringing their son, Todd, to daycare. He was killed instantly when another vehicle slammed into them on the Passenger side.

For weeks afterward Betty had tried to initiate a conversation with him but Mitchell's head was full of the torment of suddenly losing a child. It was doubly hard for Sandra, Mitchell's wife. But neither of them could look beyond their own grief. They divorced a year after their loss.

Mitchell still had work which he hung onto like a lifeline. As the Good Luck Glove Factory was sold and became the Nationwide Glove Company, with headquarters in Hong Kong, he barely noticed the change in management.

But Betty did.

She noticed the thinning of the production lines. The company had been slipping in sales for a few years, but now it accelerated. The shipping department was down to a fraction of what it had once been. She noticed the chatter in the lunchroom changed from catching up on family happenings to circulating rumors about when the factory was going to shut down.

And from the corner of her eye, she began to notice Mitchell.

She had been a friend of Sandra's. They had lunch once a week. Betty listened as Sandra described Todd's latest toddler experiences. Crawling, walking, eating solid foods. His first words. His favorite piece of clothing was a Superman t-shirt purchased at the local Superman Museum. The day he cut his first tooth.

Betty had gone to her son's funeral service at St. Rose of Lima. She had reached out to Sandra afterward at the gravesite.

"I'm so very sorry for your loss," Betty said.

Sandra looked up from the ground and their eyes met. She nodded before speaking. "I was in a hurry that morning. Didn't want to be late. Had a perfect attendance record." She laughed at the irony. "Didn't want to spoil it."

"It wasn't your fault. The newspaper said there were dozens of accidents that morning. No one was given a ticket."

"I didn't even take the time to tell my son that I loved him that day." Sandra's face was swollen with the guilt of sleepless nights. "What kind of a mother forgets to do that?"

"You didn't forget Sandra. You were trying to get to work and became distracted. It happens to all of us."

Actually, it had never happened to Betty.

She had never married or had children. She had her fair share of boyfriends in high school, but she wasn't about to arrange her life around the whims of romance. After high school she enrolled at Massac Community College, earning an associate's degree in production management. After a year working the various lines, she was promoted to assistant supervisor and then to a line supervisor position.

And the truth was that Betty was seldom distracted. Especially at work. She was a very focused person. She noticed when Sandra quit her job shortly after the funeral. She noticed when the lunchroom rumor mill described how she had moved out of state. A cousin in California had extended an invitation to try a fresh start in a new place. Betty noticed as Mitchell slowly appeared to have taken less interest in the monthly supervisory meetings. He had usually been excited to implement improvements. Took notes. Now he mostly sat and doodled through them.

This brings us back to Metropolis Bridge.

Mitchell shrugged before answering her question about him being distracted. "I wanted to give my pinkslip a proper burial, that's all."

"And you needed to jump into the river to be sure it sunk?"

"Something like that."

"Listen to me, Mitchell. What is taking your own life going to accomplish? Will it bring your son back? Will it bring your ex-wife back?"

"What is this, Tough Love 101?" He backed a bit away from the railing.

"I'm being realistic," she answered.

"So am I!" He clenched his fists.

"How is jumping into the river being realistic?"

"Life is suffering and I've had my fill of it."

"I understand pain," she said.

He looked at her before answering. "Really? You know what it's like to lose a son? To have a smiling, healthy, happy, loving kid one morning. And before the end of the day, he's gone? Without any warning? No chance to say goodbye? No chance to absorb the shock of his not being there?"

Betty shook her head.

"What would you know about the pain of a marriage gone south? The pain of your spouse being so shell-shocked that you can't shake her out of it because you're in shock yourself? Then your spouse decides that it's too painful to stay with you because you remind her of her son? And she takes off for the West Coast because the only solution she can come up with is one in which you aren't there?"

Betty remained silent, listening.

"You know what it's like growing up in a small town like this? Believing anything is possible. Even walking across this bridge on a dare, time and time again, because you felt like you were invincible? Life was yours for the taking?"

Slowly Betty looked down at the river and then back at Mitchell. "I don't know what you've gone through," she said. "But I do understand what pain feels like."

She sighed before continuing. "You and I, we're not spring chickens. We don't get to our age without getting hit in the head by life a few times. It's different circumstances, but the same pain."

Mitchell stood upright, challenging her. "Tell me then."

"You said something about growing up in a small town. And you're right. Metropolis is small enough for families to know each other. Do you remember my father?"

Mitchell shook his head no.

"That's because by the time I was four he was gone. He headed across the river to Paducah to find himself and then wound up someplace out west. Just like Sandra."

Mitchell raised his eyebrows.

"One day he got in the car and told my mom he was going to get some cigarettes. He never came back. I never saw or heard from him again. I figured I must have done something very wrong for him to leave us. Every father-daughter dance in junior high school, I stayed at home remembering how he had forgotten us. In grade school before 'bring your daughter to work day' I sat in class listening to what all the dads did until I couldn't take it anymore and ran to the bathroom to cry my eyes out."

Mitchell began to say something, but held back, realizing Betty had more to tell him.

"The feeling of emptiness from not having a father who cared for me grew. I began to search for love like my soul was aching for a drink of cold water. I began to pay attention when guys started to notice me. Sex was a way of dealing with my anger. Until my senior year of high school. One of the guys I'd been with got me pregnant. Do you remember Greg Martin?"

"The class president?" Mitchell wondered why Greg had suddenly disappeared. They weren't especially close so he had chalked it up to senioritis and moved on, not being one to hone in on hallway gossip.

Betty nodded. "Yeah. His family left town mid-way through the final semester. They put him in a private school near Evanston.

Figured he was all set to attend Northwestern anyway, so what the heck. And they gave me the money to go to a private clinic for an abortion."

"Wow." Mitchell was now truly paying attention to her.

"Two days before my abortion was scheduled I walked along this bridge and was ready to take a permanent swim in the river, just like you. But instead, I started bleeding and had a miscarriage. So I guess the joke was on him."

"I had no idea. I'm sorry."

She sighed. "I don't mean to burst your bubble, but you aren't the only one who has had hard times, Mitchell. Stick around long enough on this earth and they'll come to you."

He turned away from the railing altogether so that his entire body was facing Betty. Suddenly, he wasn't distracted by his own pain anymore.

"It's not your fault," he almost whispered.

"That's what my therapist says," out came a quick, sarcastic snap of a laugh.

"Betty, it's not your fault," he repeated the statement, slowly.

"Tell me something I don't know."

"Greg Martin was a real mud jackass."

"What?" she let out a real laugh this time.

"He was worse than an ordinary mule."

She stopped laughing and looked at Mitchell, full-on.

"He didn't appreciate your beauty. Your strength."

"I was damaged goods long before I got pregnant," Betty said. "My miscarriage was God's punishment for my sins."

He moved closer. "I don't for a second believe that."

"You're forgetting I started to bleed right here," pointing down for emphasis. "On this very bridge."

"But you didn't jump."

"I was going to!" she insisted.

"Your miscarriage isn't God's punishment for wanting to jump."

"How do you know? How can you say that?"

Mitchell put his hands on Betty's shoulders before answering. "I haven't been to church since Todd was killed. But I know the traffic accident that took him wasn't caused by God. Shirley's leaving wasn't caused by God."

"How do you know?" She insisted.

"We have free will. We have a choice in what we do. Or don't. It's up to us." He answered.

"Sort of takes God off the hook, doesn't it?"

"It's complicated," he admitted. "But I decided to come here after work today. God didn't make me."

He paused. "I'm beginning to realize something. I don't want to be here."

Betty frowned. "With me?"

"No. On this bridge." He looked at Betty again. "And I don't think you do either."

"You aren't making sense on that one. I'm only here because you were going to jump."

He shook his head. "Why did you come here, Betty?"

"I followed you."

"Maybe on one level. But I think you were following yourself. Back to your miscarriage."

She began to cry. "O.K. Hold on. I thought I was being the strong one in this scenario."

"There isn't any strong one or any scenario," he handed Betty his handkerchief. "This is life and we've both been hurt."

She wondered why Mitchell had never noticed her in the year since his divorce. They had been on the Safety Committee together. They attended the same weekly supervisor's meetings. They had attended a few after-hours gatherings with co-workers. *Is it too soon to make a move?* She had thought, *he's still grieving. I know he isn't seeing anyone. But he needs to! He's got to get that grief out somehow or it'll suffocate him.*

For his part, Mitchell slowly found himself opening up to Betty, in snippets of conversation, shared laughs, gradual trust.

When management announced the factory was closing, Betty had been standing just a few feet away from Mitchell and had seen the look on his face. It wasn't pretty. She had watched him slowly read the pinkslip over and over again. Like it was a novel.

She had been in line with him when they punched out for the day. His face was downright ashen. Right then and there she asked him if he wanted to go grab a bite to eat. He had not heard her invitation and walked right by her out the door.

But instead of rejection, she felt genuine concern.

That was Betty's usual way of going through life. She was a natural font of enthusiasm for others, easily seeing when they needed a kind word or a smile or a hug. It wasn't by circumstance that the production line she was in charge of routinely outperformed their peers.

But she had a tendency to put others' needs ahead of her own. Her adult years seemed to have been taken up by avoiding intimacy.

Until now. It was staring her right in the face.

Betty gave Mitchell a hug. "Let's both get off this bridge," she said, taking him by the hand.

Emmie Gets the Mail

"Emmie, run on down and pick up the mail. We'll have lunch ready when you get back."

To Emmie, her mom's ask was more like an invitation. After being inside doing house chores that morning, she welcomed the chance to get some fresh air.

The family farm was about three miles west of Karnak. It was far enough away from Metropolis that going into town was reserved for weekends. The farmhouse was on top of a 45-degree hill along a red clay dirt road. Their mailbox was located at the very bottom, almost 700 yards away. In 1929, rural route carriers typically delivered only along main country roads where the mailboxes were set.

As soon as Emmie shut the screen door behind her the sounds of spring became crystal clear. The bluebirds, robins, and finches were chirping up a storm. She could inhale the distinct smell of the manure that her dad, Anson, had just finished spreading across the last of his 100 acres.

Earth smells, she smiled, remembering her dad's term for it.

Emmie had several chores linked to helping her mom but, by far, the one she enjoyed the best was picking up the mail.

She had only made it from her front porch steps, past the driveway to the side road before she started to skip. As she turned to begin walking down that road Emmie started to hum "Skip to my Lou."

Skip, skip, skip to my Lou,
Skip, skip, skip to my Lou,
Skip, skip, skip to my Lou,
Skip to my Lou, my darlin'.
Fly's in the buttermilk,
Shoo, fly, shoo,
Fly's in the buttermilk,
Shoo, fly, shoo,
Fly's in the buttermilk,
Shoo, fly, shoo,
Skip to my Lou, my darlin'...

She knew the song because Emmie went with her parents and two older brothers the first Saturday of each month to the Metropolis High School gym, which hosted a line dance for the families living in town and anyone else in their part of Massac County who was interested. There was a regular band from around town that played, but anyone who came was welcome to bring along their instrument and add to the song.

Being five years old, most often Emmie danced for the first hour, inbetween helping herself from the potluck buffet table set along the side where hungry dancers could help themselves to chicken, potato salad, ham, along with fresh vegetables and casseroles. Of course, there was a separate table for desserts, including pies, cakes, tarts, and cobblers.

After having had her fill, she would usually lay down on the floor across from the dancing, and promptly fall asleep.

Emmie continued along her walk to the mailbox, by tossing a pebble into the hedgerow which Anson cut meticulously. You could pick out his property border that ran along the side road simply by eyeing it. A few yards past this particular section, towards the top of the hill, is where she spent a lot of her free time after school in late Spring, picking strawberries with her brothers, Peter and Clay.

Peter was four years older and was given to staying on task, while Clay was two years older and had a mischievous streak in him.

"Hey Em," he'd call out. "This row has extra juicy berries in it."

"Why's that?"

"Because dad spread the fertilizer on this row heavier."

He'd pick a few and hand them over to her.

"See?" he'd say. "What'd I tell you? Want to trade rows?"

Of course, Emmie shook her head `yes,' especially after eating the berries Clay had given her that were warm and so ripe, she had to wipe the juice off her chin.

In fact, there wasn't that much of a difference among any of the rows in the patch. But Clay had already picked out his row, smiling at the joke he had played on her.

Emmie kept on walking down the road until she found the large boulder that marked her neighbor's property. It was flat at the top and large enough so she could take off her sweater, spread it across, and lay down. By now the sun had warmed the rock to the point where its heat soaked into her sweater, encouraging her to linger.

She looked up at the cumulonimbus clouds lazily floating across the mid-morning sky. *That's exactly how I feel*, she thought. *I don't have a single thing to worry about.* It was Emmie's honest assessment of her life.

"Hey, Emmie!" It was her friend Amanda Eisenstadt whose family lived two farmhouses down the road.

"Emmie, get off that rock and come here!" Amanda's voice was friendly but insistent and a few decibels louder.

Emmie yawned and jumped off the rock. She had spent a good fifteen minutes staring at the sky and hesitantly looked in the direction of the familiar voice.

"Hi 'ya, Mandy!"

"Come and take a look at this!" Amanda motioned to something in the grass along the road. Just up from a ditch where water often gathered after a rainstorm. "It's a little frog."

Amanda was down on all fours and gently prodding the creature along. "See how it hops?"

"It's such a small thing," Emmie said. "Probably misses its mother."

"I don't think frogs have families," Amanda said. "At least not like we do."

Emmie shook her head. "But all animals have parents, that must mean they have sisters and brothers."

"Why would you say such a thing?"

"Because God made them. Just like he made us." Emmie said, pointing her finger at the frog.

Amanda said. "It came from a frog egg."

Emmie smiled. "But it's still part of a family."

Amanda nodded. "All of nature is one big family when you look at it that way."

"Do you know about Genesis?" Emmie went to St. Paul's Lutheran Church and their Sunday School had just finished a series on the first book of the Bible.

"What about it?" Amanda was genuinely curious. Her parents were Jewish but weren't strictly observant. During the high holy days and other important celebrations, they went across the Ohio

River to Paducah to attend synagogue services.

"Genesis is the first book of the Bible and it's all about how God created the earth," Emmie said.

"My dad is helping me read the Tanakh."

"The what?"

"The Tanakh. It's a combination of the Torah, Nebi'im, and Ketuvim. And it's got the first 39 books of your Bible. I know how God created the earth."

"You know about the Garden?"

Amanda laughed. "Yes, I know about the Garden."

"And Noah and the flood?"

Amanda nodded her head in agreement.

"Then you should know why God saved the animals!" Emmie seldom sounded so insistent.

"Because he loved all of His creation." Amanda was equally convinced.

Emmie moved a little closer to Amanda and smiled.

Amanda looked down. "Hey, it's gone!" As they were talking the little frog had inconspicuously hopped away.

"I have to go," Emmie said, standing up.

They hugged before going their separate ways.

Why is it so hard for people to believe that they're part of something bigger? Emmie thought. *If they would just look around, they'd feel it.*

She kept walking down the road until she spied Mr. Gutherson's three horses lazily eating some grass. Emmie was especially fond of Rambler, the name he had given to his best Percheron draft horse.

Rambler was instrumental to Mr. Gutherson who plowed 100 of his 120 acres, which stood about halfway down the hill to the row of mailboxes, Emmie's ultimate destination.

Emmie walked up close to the fence. "Hey Rambler!" she coaxed.

The strong horse whinnied back to his friend and came up to her.

"I've got a treat for you!" Emmie pulled out a carrot she had been saving for him.

Rambler took the carrot in his mouth, and paused a moment, looking Emmie in the eyes. When he was done eating his treat, he nudged Emmie and whinnied again.

Emmie laughed. "Sorry fella. I don't have any more."

She petted Rambler's head and ears.

"Did you know that Noah had two horses on the Ark? That's where you came from."

Rambler kept near Emmie, shaking his head as if in agreement.

"Actually, that's where all horses came after the Flood."

Emmie remembered the flannelgraph of the Flood that Miss Emery had used in teaching her Sunday School class at St. Paul's only a few weeks ago. There were about a dozen different animals represented.

"How in the world could an Ark hold two of every kind of animal?" Bobby Anderson had asked.

"God provided a huge boat," Miss Emery had answered, noting the verses in Genesis that gave the actual measurements.

It was impressive. But most all of the children in Miss Emery's class were farmers. They knew how much food their animals ate because they helped feed them every morning before school.

"That Ark couldn't have held enough space for all the food those animals would eat for 40 days," Bobby said.

"Well, you're forgetting something," Miss Emery said. "God can work miracles. And God worked several to keep that Ark afloat and the animals fed. Not to mention Noah's family. Remember there weren't any such things as iceboxes back then to keep food from spoiling."

The class nodded in agreement.

"That's where faith comes in," Miss Emery had said. "We can't really believe in anything without it can we?"

Emmie had been among the first to nod again.

To Emmie, faith was as real as the red clay road she walked down to get to the mailbox. It was as real as the fence she was leaning on as she stroked Rambler's mane. It was as real as the breeze that was kicking up in the mid-morning sky.

Just then Mr. Gutherson walked up with a feed bucket.

"This one almost missed breakfast. He got out of the barn during the night and wandered over to the lower forty." He smiled at Emmie. "Did you ever do such a thing?"

"No Mr. Gutherson. I sleep in a bedroom."

The farmer laughed and held the bucket toward Rambler. "Easy boy, take some time to breathe."

"He sure likes his oats, doesn't he?" Emmie asked.

"Oats and hay and grass and most anything else he can get ahold of," Mr. Gutherson said, petting Rambler's face. "He's a hard worker, so he deserves it."

"I'm a hard worker too!" Emmie said.

"Really?" Mr. Gutherson pretended not to know that almost every farm household along the road had someone designated to retrieve the mail each day. Usually, it was the youngest child.

"Yep. I'm on my way to pick up the mail right now."

"Well, if you're doing a chore, I don't want to keep you."

"It's alright Mr. Gutherson. Mama told me I had until lunchtime."

Mr. Gutherson took a look at the sky. "Well, I don't have my watch on me, but I'd guess it's getting close to eleven o'clock. And

I've got the farrier coming to take a look at Rambler's feet before lunch."

"Farrier?"

"Someone who checks Rambler's hooves and shoes and makes sure everything's okay down there," he explained, pointing to Rambler's feet. "Next year I'm planning to get a tractor. They're coming down in price enough so I can get one."

Emmie frowned. "What will happen to Rambler?" she asked.

"Oh, don't worry. I'm going to keep Rambler in an open pasture. Maybe some city kids will come out to meet him. Probably a lot of them haven't even seen a horse close up."

She laughed at the idea that there were kids who had never gotten close enough to a horse to pet one. "Well, I guess I better be headed along," Emmie excused herself.

"Sure thing, Emmie. Tell your parents I said howdy."

"Sure thing, Mr. Gutherson!"

Emmie kept in mind what Mr. Gutherson had said about the time, so she began to skip the rest of the way down the hill.

Right up until she met Mattie Meyers, who lived at the very bottom of the road. The Meyers' house sat near the intersection of the road Emmie had been walking down and Schoolhouse Road, which was the one the rural route carrier used to deliver the mail.

Mattie's family was well off, compared to the other farmers who lived near Karnak. Her grandfather had come to Metropolis from New York State with money. He had run a delivery business but decided to get into farming. Especially where acreage was inexpensive. He sold the business, came to Karnak, and began to buy land.

He rented most of it out and soon owned a few buildings in town, mostly near the town square.

When he and his wife passed away his oldest son moved into

the family home. Although he now lived in the country, Mattie's father had never done any farm chores in his life.

Mattie was used to the finer things in life. She wore linen dresses, whereas most of her peers wore simple gingham. She had silk gloves where most girls her age had cotton. And she wore genuine leather shoes and boots gotten when the family went to Chicago on shopping trips a few times a year. Most children from Karnak wore simple footwear from the only store in Metropolis that sold them.

Mattie had been playing in her backyard which faced the road Emmie was walking on, so she had seen her coming.

"Morning, Emmie!" she smiled, waving.

"Morning, Mattie!"

"Would you like some lemonade?"

Emmie thought a second. She was running a little behind schedule, but then, picking up the mail was a thirsty job on what was turning out to be a warm day.

"I sure would. Thanks!"

"It'll just be a minute," Mattie said, running into the house.

Emmie sat down on her porch steps.

She watched bluebirds flitting back and forth across Mattie's yard which was surrounded by acres of open farmland to attract them. It didn't hurt that Mattie's dad had also planted blueberries, black cherries, and flowering dogwood trees as well. A veritable feast for them.

"Here you go!" Mattie said, handing her a glass of lemonade.

Emmie took a long swig. "That's really good. Your mom makes it just right."

"I made it," Mattie smiled. "Most people make it too sweet. But I remembered you don't like it that way."

If she lived to be a hundred, Emmie would never forget that day in kindergarten. Miss Grunzey had made lemonade and cookies to celebrate the final day of school that year. It was early June but already hot outside. Mattie and Emmie had been taking turns in a jump-rope contest and were ready for a break.

They came inside to pour a glass of lemonade and went to sit down on the schoolhouse steps.

Almost as soon as Emmie put the glass to her lips and took a deep swallow, a frown spread across her face as she spat the rest of it out.

"Goodness!" She said under her breath. "I mean, I appreciate Miss Grunzey wanting to give us something to drink, but this has way too much sugar in it."

Emmie moved closer to Mattie and whispered. "Ought to call it sugaraide and just get it over with."

Mattie had laughed and pulled up to her friend to jump rope.

It was at that instant that Emmie and Mattie became good friends.

Emmie pulled back from the pleasant memory to continue her conversation.

"What's on your mind this morning?" Emmie asked.

"We've known each other since we've been born. I mean, we live along the same road. We go to the same school. We've been to each other's homes a thousand times. Our parents take us into town every Saturday for line-dancing at the high school."

Emmie nodded and raised her eyebrows slightly, encouraging Mattie to continue.

"Do you think we'll ever find another place as perfect as this one?"

"What do you mean?" Emmie asked. "Is somebody asking you to leave?"

Mattie laughed. "No. But I love it here. Being out in the country. But not too far away from town. And we know a lot of people and have lots of friends."

Emmie nodded again. One of her favorite things in the world was the Saturdays in summer when her relatives took turns having all the family over for picnics. They weren't fancy, held in the back-yard, with blankets spread out, and benches for the potluck-style meal. Normally it included whatever vegetables were in season (starting with lettuce and radishes and moving on to green beans, squash, corn, and tomatoes). Along with chicken, sausages, and beef. Not to mention the pies and cakes!

Usually, the picnic get-togethers lasted the entire afternoon, into the early evening, and there were at least a dozen or more cousins to play with and laugh with.

"We'll always have these memories," Emmie reassured her friend. "Always. It's just like Miss Grunzey keeps telling us, God's got each of us in the palm of his hand."

After Emmie had retrieved the mail, she bounded up the porch steps of her home, making it clear she had returned.

"Lunch is ready, Emmie!" her mother sang out.

"Coming, mom!" she answered, with a big smile on her face.

Aunt Millie and Uncle George

The house was in a state of ruin.

Windows on both floors had long ago been broken and the shattered glass lay intermeshed with layers of clothes, household items and papers strewn across the floor by the wind.

A stairwell led upstairs to the bedrooms. It had once been an elegant walnut, but weather and time had greatly eroded its character into a state of decay.

In one of the upstairs bedrooms, the bed lay curiously intact, with sheets and bedspread. The wind and rain had caused weird wrinkles to appear on it. On the floor, near a dresser, among scattered papers, lay a letter from her sister Amelia, telling Aunt Millie that a nephew had just been born back in Michigan.

Downstairs there was a Round Knob phone directory from 1938, a fragile shade of yellow. Next to the directory, there were a few photographs enclosed in broken frames – Uncle George and Aunt Millie sitting and smiling on the front porch of their home, proud and happy; Aunt Millie sitting on a horse; and three very young boys dressed in their Sunday best, looking very mischievous.

Over thirty years later from the date on the phone directory, the whole house had a sharp odor of mold and dust. Like a museum that had gone to seed.

Aunt Millie couldn't have been more than 35 years old when Uncle George died. She and Uncle George had three sons and were living on a farm about five miles northeast of Round Knob. The town consisted of a general store, a small train depot, and a grocery. It was just far enough away from Metropolis to be considered a distinct place. Seemingly set out in the middle of nowhere, completely surrounded by farmers' fields. The name was derived from a large round knoll that was used as a sledding ground when there was enough snow. Being at the very tip of southern Illinois, the relatively mild winters didn't often accommodate. But in the summer the same spot proved to be a wonderful area for a picnic.

Uncle George was tall and lanky with a thick crop of reddish-brown hair that gave him the appearance of being some sort of human weed, especially when he was dressed in his overalls, which he usually was.

The Spring before Uncle George died, he had sold his two mules and gone into Metropolis to William Standard's John Deere franchise to purchase a brand-new tractor. He was proud of the purchase because he was among the first of his farmer friends to get one.

It was May of 1947 and Round Knob was an oasis of post-war prosperity. The hamlet had sent 11 men off to war, each of them exceptionally healthy, big-boned, with firm, strong hands that had borne the brunt of knowing a hard day's work. All but one of them had returned safely home.

Springtime was a season when rich, deep aromas permeated the air around Round Knob. "Earth smells," Aunt Millie was fond of calling them. Like the sharp smell of the accumulated winter's worth of cow manure being spread across the fields; the smell of the land being plowed in preparation for planting; the sweet, clean smell of the air after a spring rain.

Early spring was a busy time as well.

Uncle George was awake at 4:30, firing up the wood-burning stove, setting a pot of coffee on top to begin the process of percolation. He was in the habit of walking in his bare feet until waking up his oldest son, Percell, to help with milking the cows.

Percell would stretch out in his bed as if his limbs were made of elastic, and he would make his way downstairs to the kitchen, turning on the radio turned to "the Chicago station," to get the day's weather report. Percell had a very wide, thin smile, just like his father's, that was overwhelmingly, crookedly shy. The smile, if it had been rounded out, could easily have encompassed his entire face, leaving some grin left to spare.

Once the coffee had started sending out its caffeinated perfume Aunt Millie was up and dressed, cooking up a breakfast of pancakes, sausage, and fried potatoes. The first meal of the day in Round Knob was usually just as big as supper because it had to supply enough energy to propel a person through six hours of hard, physical labor until noontime.

After the table was cleared the division of work began. Percell did "barn chores," which consisted of milking and feeding the few cows the family had; feeding the chicken and gathering eggs and looking after the other livestock before cutting across the neighboring farm to classes at Round Knob's one-room school, named "Button Hole." (Local kids used to call it "Butt 'n Holler" which was actually no reflection on Miss Jane Grunzey who taught there).

While Percell and his brothers were attending Button Hole School, Uncle George could usually be found somewhere outside tending to the 160 acres of land he had. It was a constant cycle of preparing, plowing, planting, weeding, and harvesting.

The particular day in May that had a lasting effect on Aunt Millie was the 10th. It was a Wednesday and it had started out cool, with a mild breeze out of the south. By noon the wind had died down and it was warm. The ground still contained a bit of moisture from the winter thaw and after recent rains, was wet, particularly in spots that weren't well-drained.

As the timepiece on the kitchen wall showed one o'clock, Aunt Millie wasn't overly concerned because this was the first day Uncle George was using the new John Deere tractor. She knew how much he loved to try out new machinery. Usually, he would break from work and head home for lunch at noon.

When two o'clock came and went, Aunt Millie broke away from her own set of chores, wrapped a couple of thickly sliced chicken sandwiches for Uncle George, hitched the family horse up and went off to deliver a late lunch to her husband.

The horse's name was Rusty, and as his name implied, he had a rich, roan color. He was not a typical farm horse, having been purchased from a traveling circus that had visited Metropolis. The circus was about to winter over in Oklahoma and the manager had decided to sell Rusty rather than pay for his off-season upkeep.

Uncle George gave the manager $20 dollars for him and helped the circus break down its tents. It turned out to be a more-than-equal exchange. In fact, Rusty proved to be an extremely reliable horse. Unusually healthy, Rusty was put to good use around the farm.

Of course, Aunt Millie called on Rusty mainly because she loved to go riding. She enjoyed going for short, spirited rides along the dirt road that took a wide turn by the family farm before it ran by a patch of bordering woods.

Rusty was eager to be regularly exercised and there was a mutual exchange of affection between horse and rider – a common bond of love for the outdoors and the freedom of movement.

It took Aunt Millie about twenty minutes to pick up the sound of the John Deere's engine running smoothly. Following the sound, she guided Rusty along to a gully that ran alongside a field Uncle George had planted in wheat.

The gully was nearly three feet deep and Aunt Millie knew something was wrong because she could hear the distinct sound of the tractor's engine close by, but she couldn't see it anywhere. Once she got to the tip of the gully and looked over, her worry was confirmed.

The tractor had tipped over somehow, and Uncle George lay face down underneath it. His left leg was somehow pinned behind the back axle.

Aunt Millie jumped off the horse, quickly turned off the tractor, picked up a rope from Rusty's saddle, tied a loop around the saddle-horn, tied a connecting knot on the tractor's seat, and coaxed Rusty to gently lift the tractor off of her husband's leg.

Uncle George's eyes had been shut but once the tractor had been lifted his eyes met Aunt Millie's and slowly, with great effort, he whispered, "Honey, I think you better get me some help."

In certain situations, the human mind has the capacity to divorce itself from conscious thought in order to automatically summon the inner strength necessary to deal with a crisis. Once Aunt Millie was back on Rusty, she had the horse moving at a gallop across the same road he had leisurely trotted over only moments before.

Aunt Millie was not aware of how she and Rusty got back to the farmhouse. She wasn't fully aware that she had called up her in-laws to ask for their help until she hung up the phone, sat down by the kitchen table, and tried very hard to keep from fainting by putting her head between her legs, breathing deeply.

Aunt Millie had spoken to Uncle George's father who was called Wester (although his Christian name was Wesley). Wester had a pick-up truck and lived on the adjoining farm, so within a few minutes he arrived in Aunt Millie's kitchen with his wife Earlene. Millie spoke in an eerily distanced tone, indicating shock.

"George is in the gully. Tractor fell over on him. I used Rusty to lift the tractor off. He needs to get to the hospital."

Wester, Earlene and Aunt Millie piled into the pick-up and together, using a section of plywood, lifted Uncle George onto the back of the truck. George was in pain, but he was coherent and insisted that he be taken back home to be washed up before going to the hospital. (The back of his pants and shirt were caked with a mixture of mud, sweat and blood, his face and hair were matted up.)

Percell and his brothers were home from school by the time Uncle George had been washed up (laying right there in the truck). Aunt Millie left Earlene in charge of the boys as she drove with Wester to Paducah – just across the Ohio River from Metropolis, where the nearest hospital was located.

Ordinarily, such a trip would be cause for gaiety. It wasn't every day that a resident of Round Knob made the trek into Metropolis, let alone to Paducah. Metropolis itself wasn't large enough of a town to support its own hospital, but compared to Round Knob, it was gigantic.

Wester's Uncle Orville ran a small diner located across the street from the town square. It was an especially popular place to spend time when school let out in the early afternoon. Orville was grateful for the after-school business, but he wasn't too patient. He grew a little tired of having to explain he had a limited choice of ice cream.

"I got chocolate and vanilla," he'd sometimes snap. "If you want anything besides a banana split, you'll have to go to Farley's." (Farley's was only a few blocks away on Market Street and boasted four kinds of ice cream, and bananas and strawberries in season.)

Once they had arrived at the hospital, Uncle George was seen by a doctor right in the lobby and was sent up to surgery from there. He had a broken leg and a collection of contusions and abrasions to the back of his head.

At the time of Uncle George's operation, the surgeon had determined that his condition appeared to be stable. Unfortunately, there was no way of telling just how exhausted his body had become from the loss of blood. He died during the night from a post-operative shock following what normally would have been a low-risk operation.

In effect, while Uncle George cleaned up before going to the hospital, his body had become increasingly unable to keep itself functioning. The operation became the last straw.

Uncle George's sense of cleanliness had cost him his life.

The night nurse on the post-surgical ward had found Uncle George dead when she responded to his roommate's knocking over a pitcher of water around four in the morning. Aunt Millie had spent the night in the hospital's surgical waiting room which had a couch in it. Within minutes of the night nurses' discovery, she was gently coaxed awake and told what had happened.

Once Aunt Millie received the news, she politely folded up a blanket a nurse had given her, handing it back with a simple "thank you," and calmly walked to the lobby to call Wester for a ride home.

Uncle George's funeral was two days later, on a Friday that was bright and sunny and full of the promise of summer. Pastor

Eberhardt of the Evangelical Church of Round Knob talked about sorrow in his sermon. He quoted from the seventh chapter of Ecclesiastes: "A good name is better than precious ointment; and the day of death than the day of one's birth..."

And he quoted Isaiah chapter 35: "...and the ransomed of the Lord shall return and come to Zion, with songs and everlasting joy upon their heads; they shall obtain joy and gladness, and sorrow and sighing shall flee away..."

Pastor Eberhardt was about five feet, five inches tall and his dark brown hair was thinning out. He wore wire-rimmed glasses and he, too, was a farmer, although on a much smaller scale than Uncle George.

Uncle George and the pastor had been good friends, and they were not above teasing each other about the current status of each other's crops. They would joke about the weather, or the St. Louis Cardinals. In fact, Pastor Eberhardt, with his thick, strong hands and stocky frame, looked more like a farmer than a preacher. He tried hard to balance God's righteousness with God's mercy in his teaching and life, and his small congregation loved him for it.

The weekend after Uncle George's funeral, Aunt Millie packed a suitcase for herself and each of her three boys and moved in with her sister, Amelia.

Aunt Millie would never set foot in her home again.

During World War II, Amelia's eldest had enlisted in the Army, followed shortly by their other son, who joined the Navy right after high school, a few months after Pearl Harbor. It was the eldest who enticed his dad to move north for a job. Because Amelia had a daughter who was still in high school at the time, Amelia decided to remain in Metropolis until she graduated.

Aunt Millie and Amelia had personalities that blended well together wonderfully, being a tonic for each other's spirits in times of crisis.

Amelia was a very prim and proper lady, enjoying wearing gingham dresses. She had a sense of humor, but it usually took a second seat to her practicality. Millie was pretty much a free spirit, with a pronounced sense of humor. She always brought out the lighter side of her sister when they were together. Millie was two years older, but relatives and friends considered Amelia "the practical one," although Millie could most definitely take care of herself.

After her daughter's graduation, Amelia moved her family to Michigan, joining her husband. After World War II, Aunt Millie and her sons followed.

On the bus ride North, Aunt Millie noticed how the rolling hills of Southern Illinois were gradually replaced by flat ground. She had never traveled so far away from her homeplace in her life. Several times along the way she had felt herself starting to cry, but she stopped when she saw the look of wonder in her boys' eyes.

Once Aunt Millie got off the bus in Battle Creek, the two sisters squealed in absolute delight before crying into each other's arms; hugging each other tightly.

Life was going to be much different, but it would still go on.

Gradually, the memories of Aunt Millie's farmhouse would not be as painful. They were replaced by the comfort of seeing so much of Uncle George in her sons.

Addie Mae and Emma

Addie Mae pushed open the door to the Metropolis Public Library and ran across the street to the gazebo that was set in the park.

She sat down on the steps and slowly lay down so that she was looking up at the beautiful southern Illinois sky.

It was mid-September. Twilight. The crickets and cicadas were trying to drown each other out.

I wish that mom didn't have to work in the glove factory, she thought. *But then, I'm grateful that this town has a place where women can work.*

The Good Luck Glove Factory was within walking distance of downtown. Almost everything was.

As the stars began to appear overhead, she was distracted from her reverie by Emma Wilson, her best friend.

"Addie, why did you stomp out like that?"

"I didn't stomp out!"

"Well, if that's not stomping then I don't know what is. Something's got you going."

"It's nothing."

"Addie, it's something. You can talk to me."

"Not this time."

"Why not?"

"Because it's not anything that you or I or anyone can fix!"

Emma had seldom seen her friend so adamant. Under normal circumstances Addie was as even-tempered as they came, being the only daughter of a farming couple who had lived near Round Knob. The O'Neills had moved into town because Addie's dad had gotten a severe case of heatstroke and could no longer farm.

Her mom was currently working at the factory for the extra income it provided while her dad was on the mend. He was adjusting to working in the small hamburger place next to the town's movie theatre.

"Just tell me what needs fixing," Emma was desperate to understand.

Addie Mae turned her attention from the night sky to look into the eyes of her friend. She saw nothing but compassion.

"It's this town." She began. "It's eating up my imagination."

This was pretty heavy stuff to be considering. But then, Addie Mae and Emma were seniors in high school. It had been nine months since Pearl Harbor.

Almost all of the senior boys had enlisted and most all of them of age were eager to get into the military right after graduation.

"There's a war on," Emma said. "We aren't living in a normal time, in case you hadn't noticed."

Addie held her friend's right arm. "What's normal, Emma? I mean, for Metropolis. Is it spring planting and having a date for the dance on Friday night? Or going to the movies with friends on a Saturday? Or telling your mom you're going to the library to study when you're really going to slip out and get a banana split with your friends?"

"It's all of those things!"

"Doesn't a world war make you nervous?" Addie asked.

"I talk to God about it."

"When?"

"During church mostly," Emma answered.

"I'd find that too distracting."

Emma had invited her friend to church plenty of times. But Addie Mae mostly stuck to her Catholic roots at St. Rose of Lima. The core of both services was similar, but the two religions didn't encourage mixing.

Emma was one hundred percent German. Her grandparents had emigrated from the old country in the 1800s. In the beginning, the German folk mostly stuck together on family farms outside of the city, forming St. Paul's Lutheran Church with a German-speaking congregation.

Addie Mae was also one hundred percent, but Irish. Her grandparents had emigrated from the North, near Connemara, during the Potato Famine. Her grandfather was fortunate to have a cousin who had quickly moved on from New York, and settled on a farm near Karnack.

The humidity of Massac County in full summer was unlike anything either the Irish or German immigrants had experienced. But the acres upon acres of rich farmland made up for it. To someone who was used to farming, the tip of Southern Illinois was extremely attractive.

While Addie was the only daughter, she had two older brothers, Collin and Ronan, who had helped with most of the farm chores before the move into town. Their hair was black; Addie's was red. They all had thick hair that burst out in uncontrollable waves.

"Well, you've got to find a place to talk to God about it, Addie!"

"The world is changing. Faster than we can imagine. Kids from our town who would have grown up, lived and died within 50 miles of here are now fighting overseas."

"I know."

"And that doesn't frighten you?"

Emma hugged her friend before continuing. "No. I can't control the world."

"But you're not concerned about how this could all wind up?"

"I'm concerned, Addie, but I'm not afraid."

"You're still planning to go to Purdue after graduation then?"

Emma had a huge academic appetite. It expressed itself in excellent study habits, which had led to several scholarship offers.

"Yes."

Addie smiled. "You were never the traditional housewife type, were you?"

"I'm too practical to think that all my desires are going to be met by getting married. You were always the romantic one!"

"I still am. But it's a little harder to dream nowadays."

Emma laid down on the gazebo steps next to Addie.

For a good five minutes neither one spoke, perfectly content to stargaze.

Addie broke the silence. "I admire your faith. You don't seem to get frazzled as easily as I do."

"That's not so much faith as it is temperament. I was born with a slower emotional metabolism."

"Really?"

"Having German roots helps. No one is emotional in my family."

"So, just because I'm Irish I fly off the handle?"

"No. But take a look at our history together."

"Like, for instance?"

"Well, for instance, who held you back from smacking Dillon Franklin when he didn't ask you to the prom last year?"

"Dillon had it coming. He was supposed to be my boyfriend. But, ok."

"And who had to talk you out of going toe-to-toe with Mr. Sanders over your geometry exam grade?"

"He plays favorites. But I'll give you that one too."

"Need we mention the flat tire incident from earlier this summer?"

Addie sat up straight. "Come, on Emma. That's a low blow!"

"You were going to toss your bike into the Ohio River."

"I was fed up."

"We were halfway across the bridge to Paducah, Addie!"

"That was exactly the point."

"What point?" Now Emma was sitting up.

"We were halfway across and a flat-tired bike wasn't getting us anywhere."

"Do you see a pattern here?" Emma was a seasoned member of the Metropolis High School debate team.

"I can't say that I do."

"Getting caught up in the moment?"

Addie stared hard at her friend. They had been through a lot together. They had gone to the same schools since first grade. Including the Button Hole one-room schoolhouse halfway between Round Knob and Karnak that was no longer in use.

The mere thought of Button Hole caused Addie to laugh out loud.

"Now what?" Emma asked.

"Do you remember the day Miss Grunzey accidentally stepped on some dog doo-doo during recess? Her shoes were full of it."

"And as she walked up to the front of the class, she asked, `What is that smell?'"

"Rudy Meyers started to laugh. He couldn't help himself. Which only further upset poor Miss Grunzey."

"She asked him to explain what was so funny."

"He told her to look at the bottom of her shoes. When she did, her face turned redder than a beet!"

"Miss Grunzey took off her shoes and dropped them out the front side window and taught the rest of the afternoon barefoot."

Both girls looked at each other and laughed uncontrollably.

"Why do we have to grow up anyway?" Emma asked, wiping away the tears from her eyes. "I truly don't see any advantage to it."

"Eight months from now we'll be done with high school."

"What are you going to do?"

"For starters, I'd like a one-way ticket to New York City for a graduation present."

Addie had been to St. Louis once on a family trip. They had stayed in a hotel near downtown. It was her first experience riding on an elevator. She had strolled through a city with a downtown that had a dozen movie theaters - and at least that many places to eat in a three-block radius alone.

The first night in town her family ate Chinese food. She had never tasted anything like it.

Since it was summertime, they took in an outside concert by the St. Louis Symphony Orchestra. It was magnificent. Addie had played violin in the high school orchestra. They held two concerts each year. But that was nothing compared to what her ears and heart experienced that day in Lafayette Park. Not to mention the museums!

St. Louis was the nearest big city to Metropolis. And it had sparked her spirit of adventure which remained unquenchable ever since.

Addie's brothers, Collin and Ronan, were overseas. They had both enlisted. Collin in the Army. Ronan in the Navy. While she missed them, she also was a little envious that they were thousands of miles away from home. Neither one had seen much of the world outside Massac County.

Addie was bursting at the seams. She and Emma were standing on the cusp of adulthood. For all practical purposes, they were inches away from it. The fact that there was a world war on only accentuated the reality of growing up.

All around them people were growing up in a hurry. Addie saw it in the eyes of the boys who left Metropolis headed for their induction into the military. She knew most of them and their families. Among them were a few cousins. The same ones who used to play hide-and-seek and tag on lazy Sunday afternoons growing up together. Right after church, they went home long enough to change into their play clothes, grab side dishes and go to their grandparents' farms.

Families took turns, alternating locations so no one had the burden of hosting or cleaning up alone. Each farm had a huge front and back lawn with plenty of room for the children to laugh and play. The adults had more than enough room to set the spread of fried chicken, potato salad, green beans, tomatoes, and garden greens. After the main meal, the kids helped to churn the home-made ice cream, served with plenty of cake.

For Addie, this was normal. Even during the darkest days of the Great Depression, when her family was still on the farm, they had enough.

But it was different now.

There wasn't a person in Metropolis who didn't have a relative, friend or neighbor who was serving in the military or knew someone who was. It made what was going on overseas personal. When residents were asked to buy War Bonds, they did. Anyone in town who wasn't a farmer dug up patches in their backyards to grow Victory Gardens. In such a small, tight-knit community there were very few complaints about the use of gas coupons. And even though Metropolis was a sleepy river-boat town, miles away from anything strategic, city officials still practiced air raid drills.

"What's waiting for you in New York, Addie?"

"It's not one thing exactly. It's all of the possibilities."

"For instance?"

"It would be fun to work in a publishing house. I'd start out as a secretary, then become an editor. Every day I'd take the subway to work and in the evening I'd go home and work on my novel."

Addie was editor of the high school yearbook and the school newspaper. She also wrote a weekly column for the daily newspaper, called "Metropolis Minded."

"Or I could play the violin as a street musician."

"I've never heard of a woman playing their violin on the street!" Emma was adamant to keep her friend grounded in reality.

"I wouldn't play solo," Addie explained. "I'd become friends with another violinist, or someone who played the flute. Maybe even start a quartet or chamber group."

"There must be hundreds of street musicians in New York - practically one on every corner."

Addie laughed. "But they wouldn't play as well as us!"

"You're impossible."

Then, from seemingly out of nowhere, a scripture came to Addie. "'The things of the spirit can't be discerned by the natural man.'"

"What?"

"It's in the Bible. Paul's first letter to the Corinthians. We were discussing it a few weeks ago in Religion Class."

Although there wasn't a Catholic school in Metropolis, Addie's parents had made it a priority for each of their kids to attend weekly religion classes held at St. Rose of Lima.

"What was his point?"

"Our natural, practical, common-sense brain can't understand the spiritual world. It's beyond logic. We have to lean on the Spirit."

"I don't understand you sometimes," Emma sighed. "I truly don't. I mean, you don't seem that interested in talking things over with God. But you have a sensitive soul."

Addie shook her head and looked straight into Emma's eyes. "Just because I don't stick to a traditional way of doing things doesn't mean I don't believe in God. What are your plans? What will you study at Purdue?"

"I love biology and natural science. I would love to get a job doing research somewhere. Transfer to Hopkins Marine Station if I'm lucky enough to get accepted."

Hopkins is a branch of Stanford University and was established in the late 19th Century. Growing up on the banks of the Ohio River had spawned Emma's interest in aquatic life. From the time she was a child, she explored the surrounding area whenever her dad went fishing there or on Mermet Lake.

"You've always loved the outdoors!"

"And I don't mind getting my hands dirty. Or wearing waders. There's so much to be found in a river or lake. Just imagine what you can find in an ocean, Addie! It's limitless."

"So, that's why it's easier for you to go the traditional route? I mean, with religion? You see God scientifically. Down to earth."

Emma laughed. "I suppose that's true. For me, God's in the details. Right down to the cells. God's in it all."

Being scientifically minded, Emma was very familiar with the Scopes "monkey" trial. It had taken place 17 years before in Dayton, Tennessee.

The core of the case concerned John Scopes, a science teacher in a public high school who let himself be accused of teaching evolution so that he could be taken to court. William Cullen Bryan was the lawyer for the prosecution, while none other than Clarence Darrow defended Scopes.

Scopes was found guilty of violating the Butler Act, which made it unlawful to teach evolution in any state-funded school in Tennessee. But the case was dismissed on a technicality (because the judge imposed the fine on Scopes, which was the jury's job).

While the trial was viewed by many as a publicity stunt, it nonetheless caused educators to take a closer look at whatever was written in science books about evolution.

As far as Emma was concerned, her faith in God didn't rest on any scientific principle and she saw no conflict between the two.

She was logical. She loved getting to the heart of things. She was a firm believer, along with the Old Testament prophet Micah, that when it came right down to it, what the Lord required from us was "to do what is right, to love mercy, and to walk humbly with your God."

"Following God shouldn't be so difficult," Addie said.

"I agree!"

"You do?"

"Of course. Even Paul, who loved a good debate, let us in on the answer to the mystery."

Now she had Addie's full attention. "He did?"

"Sure. In the book of Colossians. He says that the mystery to the whole thing is that: 'Christ dwells in you.'"

For some reason, Addie burst out laughing at this news.

"What's so funny?"

"It's like a spiritual joke. Except that it's not."

"Right."

"So why do we have so many branches of the one true faith?"

"Maybe because we don't pay attention to the Beatitudes."

"As in, blessed are the meek and the peacemakers and all those others?"

"Pretty much."

Addie laid back down on the Gazebo steps and Emma soon followed. For a while, they were both content staring up at the night sky again.

"How many stars are in the sky?" Addie asked.

"Over a million in the Milky Way. And there are probably thousands of other galaxies out there with a million stars each."

"Wow!"

"Yeah. Wow!"

"I can't even imagine how small our little, tiny portion of the universe is. But at the same time, it's the most enormous thing we know."

Emma nodded in agreement. "Sort of like God."

"How so?"

"There's another scripture that says that we can know the Creator through what the Creator made."

"In a way, the sky is an object lesson."

"Exactly!"

There on the gazebo, across the street from the public library, the two friends held hands.

"I'm going to miss you," Addie spoke first. "I'm going to miss having conversations like this."

"Me too."

"But we'll write letters to each other."

"Long ones," Emma promised.

A Farm Family

Southern Illinois in the summer months can be downright disagreeable. At least if you weren't born into high humidity. Like Casey Madigan, who was raising two daughters after his wife, Shirley, passed away soon after giving birth to Eve, their youngest.

From early on, Eve was true to her name. Full of life. Curious. Willing to pitch in with the farm chores, of which there were plenty.

When she turned eight, she was assigned to milking the cows, feeding the chickens and gathering the eggs. These were the daily "outdoor" chores. The "inside" chores, which had started when she was five, included helping to set the table for meals and cleaning up afterward.

Because there were chores in the afternoon, the girls went home right after school. There wasn't time for childhood dawdling when supper had to be made, followed by their homework.

The family farm was located northeast of Metropolis on Massac Creek Road. The creek ran through their property, roughly dividing its 80 acres in half. The land was fertile and Casey grew corn, alfalfa, and wheat on it. He sold the grains to nearby farmers who raised livestock.

He also rented out twenty of his acres to farmers who grew crops.

Casey was a hard worker and he expected the same from his daughters.

Believe it or not, it was in the family's barn that Eve first began to dance.

It started simply. After milking the cows, she took the buckets away from the stalls and twirled around for a few minutes before emptying the buckets into the tin cannisters where the milk was kept before pick up.

When she was in high school, Eve and her older sister were permitted to go into town to the dances held on Saturday nights at the high school gym.

The gym's wooden floors felt like a magic carpet to her. At first, it was simple attraction to move with the rhythm of the music. This was the 1940s; the era of the Big Band. Even if it was Metropolis' version, it was still good enough. More often than not, the Madigan sisters danced with each other. Perfectly content to be transported off the farm, for a little while.

When Eve's sister, Caitlin, was away at college, Eve started attending the dances alone. By sophomore year she started accepting rides from Mally Roach. Like Eve, he was a sophomore at Metropolis High. Unlike Eve, he was on the shy side, even though his father ran the *Metropolis Sun* – the city's daily newspaper.

For Eve, free time was a precious commodity. What little she had of it was spent taking dancing lessons in town from Miss SuEllen Frost. On the other hand, Mally played sports: basketball in the winter and track in the spring. The boy had a natural stride and enormous energy.

It was in their sophomore year that Eve broke the conversational ice. She was headed down the first-floor hallway of the school at an uncharacteristically fast pace. As she turned the corner, she ran smack into Mally, who was standing still in front of his locker, deciding if he wanted to eat the rest of his homemade lunch before heading to practice.

The force of Eve's momentum almost knocked Mally off his feet.

"Hey!" He blurted out, turning to see who had hit him.

Eve's cheeks turned crimson. "I am so sorry!"

Mally began to sink to the floor.

"Woah! What's happening?" she asked.

Mally looked up at her and slowly spoke. "You almost knocked the wind out of me."

She sat down next to him. Luckily most of the other kids had already left the building.

"I need to watch where I'm going, don't I?" she smiled at him, noticing his thick, black hair and black eyes.

"You need to slow down."

"I'm very, very sorry. I have to get home right after school and do farm chores." She tried her best to explain her predicament.

"I know plenty of farmers and they don't go around running into people." He tried to stand up, but Eve put her hand on his shoulder.

"You should probably stay down for another minute," she advised. "You look pale. I'll stay with you."

At this point, Mally couldn't help but appreciate Eve's auburn hair and hazel eyes, plus her warm smile. He also noticed the genuine look of concern on her face.

"Don't worry," he smiled. "But if I start to die, could you do me a favor and drag me out of this building?"

Eve laughed so hard she snorted. "Wouldn't that be absolutely horrible?"

He began laughing as well.

"You can probably stand up now," she said.

Eve explained that normally she would have gotten a ride home with her sister. But her sister had moved away from home to attend college, leaving Eve on her own for a ride. She was headed toward the front of the school to see if she could catch a ride when she bumped into Mally.

"So, you still need a ride?" he asked.

"Yes. If I don't want to walk a few miles home," she admitted.

Mally took out the remains of his lunch and closed the locker door. "Come on. I'll take you home, if you don't mind riding in a Dodge DeSoto."

Eve laughed. "I don't care what kind of car it is, as long as it's got an engine that works!"

Less than a week later, the subject of her encounter with Mally came up at SuEllen's dance studio.

"He was a perfect gentleman," Eve began. "Especially since I almost knocked him over in the hall."

SuEllen was smart and practical. After graduating from the University of Illinois at Champaign-Urbana, she decided to come back to Metropolis and start up a dance studio. She had majored in dance with a secondary degree in education. It was a perfect fit for her.

"Well, his behavior is even more commendable, given how you two met," SuEllen began. "And the offer to get you home. That's icing on the cake. Mally is definitely a keeper. I mean, if you still have an interest in him."

"Oh, I do!" Eve smiled. "But he's really not much of a talker. And I'm not at all interested in sports."

"Does he have interests outside of track and basketball?" SuEllen asked.

"I'm not sure."

SuEllen whistled. "Well, there's a conversation starter if ever I came across one."

The next school year, Mally was offering a ride home to Eve regularly. Eve's sister graduated and it was a big help to free up the family car. Casey needed it, having started a farm supply store in town.

It was early spring in Metropolis. The lilacs were in full, magnificent bloom. A row of them had been planted near the High School's front entrance.

Eve and Mally were sitting on the front steps, lazily catching some sun during their lunch break.

"This is my favorite time of year," she announced.

"Mine too!" Mally agreed. "Track season practice has already begun. We're running circuits around town. Builds up endurance."

She turned to him, full face. "Why don't you ever go to the Saturday night dances? They're a lot of fun!"

"Can't dance," he explained, shrugging his shoulders.

"But it's good exercise. Plus, a nice way to get to know people."

Mally looked a little confused. "I already know a ton of people from track and basketball."

"Maybe you could expand your horizons a little bit?"

"I have. I'm considering cross country in the fall!"

Eve shook her head. "I meant your social circle, Mally."

"I really can't dance. At all."

"Have you ever tried it?"

Mally shook his head.

"Well, I bet you'd be good at it. You're an athlete. You have a sense of timing and rhythm, right?"

"I suppose."

"That's all you need to dance."

She stood up and offered Mally her hand. "Come on!"

He took it.

They faced each other as Eve helped pull him up. "Now, all you have to do is follow my lead. When I make a step, you go with me."

She began to hum the opening to "The Blue Danube" waltz, forming a square with her feet.

"See? It's simple."

After a few minutes she stopped and smiled.

"You've just taken your first dance lesson! Now all you have to do is take me to the dance this Saturday."

From that point on, Mally and Eve went to the Saturday dances together. They didn't consider themselves to be a "couple." But it was clear that they were having a lot of fun, minus any social pressure of officially dating.

And so it went, up to their senior year at Metropolis High School.

On December 22, 1941 Mally and Eve had the most serious lunchtime chat of their young lives. Christmas break was one day away. It was two days after President Franklin Delano Roosevelt announced changes to the Selective Training & Service Act, making all men between the ages of twenty and forty-four eligible for military service. Men between the ages of eighteen and sixty-four were required to register for the draft.

"So, what are you going to do now, Mally?"

He cleared his throat before answering. "Well, I'm not waiting until I'm drafted. I'm more inclined to enlist straight out of high school."

Even though she half-expected this would be Mally's course of action, Eve was still taken aback by it.

"Do you have to be so quick about it?"

Mally put his hand on Eve's. "I'm just being practical. I've already been to the Navy recruiter and he offered me a better deal than the Army ever could."

"Deal?"

Mally nodded. "I'm almost guaranteed my first choice. I'm thinking of signing up for the Signal Corps. I'll learn about electronics, which is up and coming."

"Up and coming?" Eve frowned. "There's a war on. You could get killed."

"So could millions of other guys," he countered. "I'm not unique."

"You are to me, Mally Roach!"

Eve wanted to scream, but quickly realized that it wouldn't change Mally's mind. She realized something else. She was on the cusp of falling in love. As far as she was concerned, falling in love meant that your level of caring for someone was linked to your adrenalin flow.

This was a new experience for Eve. Her mother's death so soon after her birth meant that Eve had no chance to bond with her, as she grew up. There were to be no mother-daughter talks, or the experience coming from example to guide the transition from girl to woman. And while Eve and her sister had been close growing up, the two were in the same boat when it came the lack of maternal influence.

Which brings us back to SuEllen, who had remained Eve's dance instructor throughout high school.

"There's a war on, Eve," SuEllen explained. "Try to see it from Mally's point of view."

"Yeah," Eve sighed. "He says he's being practical."

"And he is. Guys being guys, they are chomping at the bit to enlist. It's only going to get worse."

"Get worse?"

"Yes," SuEllen gently placed her hands on Eve's shoulders. "The way the war is shaping up, in a few months hundreds of thousands of men will be signing on the bottom line to get into the military. Those who sign up later, when we're in the thick of it, aren't as likely to get their choice of options."

"How do you know this stuff?" Eve frowned.

"Because I grew up in a military family. Once you sign up, it doesn't matter what a recruiter promises you. It totally depends upon your aptitude and what they need."

Eve began to cry softly.

"Mally is getting into this with his eyes open. He's just being realistic. It sounds like he's also looking ahead to when this awful war is over."

Eve pulled out a handkerchief and wiped her eyes. "For a farmer's daughter, I sure didn't pick up the down-to-earthiness of everyday living," she said.

"Honey," SuEllen spoke softly. "Dancers aren't inclined to be practical people. I'm the exception for having a double major in education with dance. That's why you and I are intergenerational soul mates!"

"So, what am I supposed to do?" Eve looked directly into SuEllen's eyes. "Just sit back and watch Mally sign up? Be the good, supportive girlfriend?"

SuEllen smiled. "It's girlfriend, is it?"

Eve slowly nodded.

Meanwhile Mally was having his own conversation with Ted Wilson, the track coach at Metropolis High. He was forty-seven years old and had been a coach for fifteen years.

"Mr. Wilson, I feel it's my patriotic duty to signup right after graduation."

Ted nodded.

"But Eve just doesn't get it."

"Should she have to?"

Mally looked at Mr. Wilson. "What do you mean?"

"Mally, if you're looking for her approval so you can enlist, it's probably not realistic. And it's placing a burden on her."

"Burden? Isn't support important?"

Ted nodded. "But you're putting her in a very awkward position. In a few months, you'll both be finished with high school. That's a huge step. She needs time to figure out what's next."

"The war! That's what's next!" Mally was adamant.

"Maybe for you. But it's not going to be the same for her," Ted cautioned. "Enlistment for you means adventure and duty. Enlistment for her means separation and the pain of not knowing if you're safe."

"I'll be fine."

Ted placed his hand on Mally's shoulder. "You don't know that for sure, son. Recruiters don't specialize in telling you what combat is like." Ted knew what he was talking about. As a young man he had seen action in WWI, towards the end.

"Look, son, war is full of death and disease. A nation doesn't gear up for war by educating its citizens about the horror of it. It's a sad thing, because it leaves each generation afterwards blind to its true costs. If you don't go along with it, you're called unpatriotic, or worse."

"Were you a dissenter?" Mally asked, point blank.

Ted shook his head. "I signed up right out of high school, just like you're wanting to do. Back then it was trench warfare. Ugly, awful stuff."

What Ted didn't tell Mally was that he had been awarded a Medal of Honor for bravery after taking over a gunnery position for a fallen soldier. He saved the lives of those in his bunker while doing so.

Eve and Mally had agreed to go for a walk early in the day on December 24th.

They met on the steps of the Metropolis Library, which was closed for the holiday. But all around them last-minute Christmas shoppers were already headed purposefully around town, looking for bargains.

They chose to avoid as much of the holiday activity as possible by crossing Metropolis Street, walking through Washington Park until they came to St. Rose of Lima Church, which had a nativity scene in front.

"It's beautiful," Eve began.

"And encouraging," Mally added.

"How so?"

"Well, to begin with, Mary and Joseph had just traveled from Nazareth to Bethlehem while she was nine months pregnant. They show up in town during a census. It's not like there were a lot of hotels back then and every available room was taken."

Eve looked at Mally. "He must have been exhausted from the stress."

Mally nodded. "So was she. Big time."

They stood silently admiring the scene for a moment.

"Can you imagine the faith they must have had?" she continued the conversation. "First-time parents. Far from home. Completely at the mercy of strangers, and their baby is God's son."

"How could they have begun to tell anyone what they were experiencing?" Mally shook his head, almost whispering.

Both Mally and Eve had grown up going to church with their families. Eve at St. Rose of Lima. Mally at First United Methodist Church.

"I wonder how much Mary knew," Eve mused. "Gabriel told her that she was going to carry God's son. And that her son would somehow redeem the world. But I don't think she knew how much he'd suffer."

"She knew Jesus was God in human form. I mean, she wound up asking him to work a miracle at the wedding feast at Cana," Mally added. "And she also sent the rest of her kids to fetch him one time, when she sensed that things were about to come to a head."

"What other kids?" Eve questioned.

"Jesus wasn't the only baby Mary and Joseph had," Mally said, matter-of-factly.

His response took Eve by surprise. "You don't believe in the Holy Family?"

Mally shook his head. "I think that's pretty much a Catholic thing, Eve. Sort of a preoccupation with the immaculate aspect of the immaculate conception."

Eve raised her eyebrows.

"Think about it," Mally continued. "Joseph and Mary were fully human. And they loved each other. Plus, there was a huge cultural disposition towards having children. Especially in Middle-Eastern culture. The more kids you had, the bigger the blessing you had from God."

"You didn't snooze your way through Sunday School, did you?" she teased.

Mally laughed. "I was really interested in all those people in the Bible. To me they were more than stories. Those guys were real, just like you and me."

"Have you ever been inside a Catholic church?" Eve asked.

"No. It's not exactly encouraged."

Eve took Mally's hand. "Well, come on. I'm encouraging you to come in with me."

They walked up the stairs, into the sanctuary. Sitting in silence for a few minutes, until Mally spoke up.

"When you really think about it, we're a lot like Mary and Joseph."

Eve's eyes grew wide. "What in the world are you talking about?"

Mally continued. "They were starting on a journey that seemed impossible to both of them. I mean, Mary had a million questions on her mind. Some angel had visited her nine months before and now she's about to have a baby. And Joseph, good night! He's racking his brain trying to figure out how he's going to be a dad to the creator of the universe! Can you imagine!"

Eve shook her head before speaking. "She was given a supernatural ability to trust. What would it be like for a first-time mom to give birth in a barn? If this was how their marriage was starting out, what was the rest of it going to be like?"

"But she trusted," Mally agreed. "Because she knew God." Mally reached out and held Eve's hand. "And we should too."

"I'm afraid that after you enlist, I'll never see you again," Eve admitted.

"I'm afraid too," Mally said. "But this is something I've got to do."

"Why is fighting always the answer?" Eve questioned. "Why hasn't the human race come up with something better? I mean, since the stone age, we keep on inventing weapons that kill more people. And we keep going into wars that promise this one will be the last."

"You must have been paying attention in history class," Mally smiled.

"Well, unfortunately, as far as the military goes, nothing has changed."

"I take it you're a pacifist?" Mally still had his hand on Eve's.

She shook her head. "I'm a realist. At least when it comes to war. I'm beginning to understand how ridiculous it is."

"But what about honor?"

Eve took her hand off of Mally's. "Who says there is anything honorable about killing innocent people? Destroying cities and homes?"

So sat Eve and Mally: Right there, in the middle of St. Rose of Lima's sanctuary, in the heart of Metropolis, on Christmas Eve.

And slowly, ever so slowly, Mally turned towards Eve.

"You want to know something? I think you're about the bravest person I know," she said.

"I feel the same way about you, Eve."

She swallowed hard before responding. "My mother died before I could have any memory of her," she said softly. "I don't handle separation very well."

Ever so slowly, they looked up at the Christmas decorations surrounding the altar and put their arms around each other.

Button Hole School

Rudy Meyers was seldom caught daydreaming. But on an early November day in 1946, his thoughts were of an automatic milking machine, yet to be invented. It would be attached to the udders of each of the ten cows he was responsible for on his father, Stefan's dairy farm in Round Knob, Illinois.

An automatic milking device would have saved the boy from having to get up so early, especially now that winter's grip was not far away. When Rudy dreamed of the machine, it came complete with rubber tubing that led all the way to the cooler, which would contain a series of electric switches to turn the suctioning on right from his bed.

Stefan Meyers owned twenty of the cows and had split the milking duties with his son. But since Stefan had a multitude of other chores, often enough the milking went entirely to Rudy, which explained why the idea of an automatic machine was so appealing.

The 11-year-old boy was in his final year at the Button Hole one-room schoolhouse that was set on McDivott Road. Rudy was in the sixth grade and he was looking forward, with a bit of anxiety, to transferring to the 'city junior high' in Metropolis, about six miles away.

Miss Jane Grunzey was entering her seventh year of teaching at the school. She was 28 years old and had come to Round Knob by way of Indianapolis. Under ordinary circumstances Miss Grunzey was a very patient teacher, but Rudy was about to be caught in the middle of another of a week-long series of daydreams.

The rest of the students in row six were completing a penmanship exercise when Miss Grunzey calmly walked up beside Rudy.

"Would you like to join the rest of the sixth graders in what we're doing, or do you have other plans for the rest of the morning?" she asked, without a trace of sarcasm.

Rudy sat bolt upright and gave Miss Grunzey a sheepish smile.

"I'm sorry ma'am," he apologized. "I didn't mean to neglect my lesson."

Suzanne Bazlee was barely able to stifle a laugh.

She sat directly behind Rudy. She had a wide-openness about her that prevented her from being discreet. Luckily, her expressiveness of personality was balanced with a tender heart that did not seek to embarrass or draw attention to another person's faults. So, instead of laughing, Suzanne decided to tease Rudy privately during lunch recess.

After the correction was given, Miss Grunzey continued walking up to the front of the classroom.

She was five foot, three inches tall but the demeanor with which she taught made her seem much taller. Miss Grunzey had blue-green eyes, the color of a lake on a summer's day when the sky overhead was cloudless. They were unusually piercing and had an almost magnetic quality.

This was Miss Grunzey's last year at Button Hole School because the Metropolis School Board had incorporated the Round Knob system into its jurisdiction. They had voted to discontinue operating the little one-room schoolhouse.

The process of incorporating the communities surrounding Metropolis had begun in the early 1940's, but it had been put on hold during the War. As gasoline and tires became accessible again, transportation for the Metropolis school system soon resulted in a fleet of buses that were quickly making it possible for children in rural areas to attend centralized schools in the city.

For Miss Grunzey, her stay in Round Knob had been one of intense pleasure. She had been born and bred in the city, but her heart was most definitely in the country. Her mother's sister had settled in Metropolis so she was very familiar with the surrounding area. When the Button Hole position became available, Miss Grunzey had jumped at the opportunity.

Across the country one room schoolhouses were becoming a rarity. The trend towards consolidation was clearly there, but for an educator, a school like Button Hole presented a unique challenge. How were you to teach 25 students, divided into six grades? How was a person to plan lessons geared to be taught in an almost simultaneous fashion?

For an ordinary teacher, this would have been a nightmare, but for Miss Grunzey it was exactly what fueled her through most of her 20's. She had come to Round Knob on the eve of her 21st birthday and had not regretted it.

Her weekday structure was unwavering. She got up at six o'clock, put on a pot of coffee and hitched up her horse, Nashville. Miss Grunzey lived in the old Parker farmhouse only a mile away from the Round Knob general store. She took Nashville into the village and brought the morning's *Chicago Tribune*, which had been dropped off at the train depot in the wee hours of the morning.

Back at home, Miss Grunzey continued her routine by mixing up a batch of biscuits to go along with the scrambled eggs she was making. Since this sort of breakfast could be fixed rather quickly, it left time for a leisurely stroll through the pages of the *Tribune.* She largely ignored the city news as she focused on national and international events. Such was the interest of a teacher who wanted to keep her lessons crisp and up-to-date.

The school day began at eight-thirty. Miss Grunzey would open the door by eight, then start the fire in the wood-burning stove in the middle of the room. She wrote out the morning's lesson plan on the chalkboard which stretched out, like two gigantic arms, to enfold two sides of the school room.

Starting the fire was one of the rules the State of Illinois had instituted in 1915 for all its teachers in one-room school-houses. Although it had been decades since the rules had been published, Miss Grunzey abided by many of them. They were as follows:

1. You will not marry during the term of your contract.

2. You are not to keep company with men.

3. You must be home between the hours of 8 p.m. and 6 a.m. unless attending a school function.

4. You may not loiter downtown in ice cream stores.

5. You may not travel beyond the city limits unless you have the permission of the chairman of the board.

6. You may not ride in a carriage or automobile with any man unless he is your father or brother.

7. You may not smoke cigarettes.

8. You may not dress in bright colors.

9. You may not, under any circumstances, dye your hair.

10. You must wear at least two petticoats.

11. Your dresses must not be any shorter than 2 inches above the ankle.

12. To keep the school room neat and clean, you must sweep the floor at least once daily, scrub the floor at least once a week with hot, soapy water, clean the blackboards at least once a day and start the fire at 7 a.m. so the room will be warm by 8 a.m.

To Miss Grunzey, these rules served more as a reminder of the importance of tradition, especially in a small town. She wasn't one to loiter in ice cream stores, dye her hair, or wear two petticoats or smoke. She understood the importance of choosing her battles. So she fought for a solid education and the choices that would eventually come for the girls she taught.

There was a sense of order which came in writing the outline for what would serve as the basis for the day's learning. It was peaceful at eight o'clock, before the children came filing in Button Hole. Since practically all of the students were living on their parents' farms, they had been up since early morning, milking, feeding, gathering eggs and helping out with other chores that could be completed before school began.

In Round Knob there was no such thing as a 'morning person.' If the morning hours were not your cup of tea, you got up anyway and learned how to bear with facing the world while half asleep. Miss Grunzey's class had learned from the example of their parents, so they didn't have to be coaxed into waking up. If they stumbled out of bed, their slumber was soon broken by the chores they did, which involved pecks from chickens, nips from a horse, or an attempted kick from an overly sensitive cow.

Above and beyond Rudy's desire for help with milking, his mind may have succumbed to the spell of daydreaming because he, too, would soon be leaving Button Hole School.

Most of his life had been spent on the family farm in Round Knob and, although he had made regular trips to town to help his father pick up supplies or visit relatives, he did not feel completely at ease in the city.

Suzanne Bazlee, being in sixth grade, was also going to be facing the change to junior high school, but she felt excited and extremely happy about it. Unlike Rudy, she was used to spending time in her grandfather's five-and-ten-cent store in Metropolis.

"I can't wait for school to begin next year," she told Rudy. "I mean, I'm not knocking the country life, but there is so much more out there."

"Like, for instance?" Rudy's eyebrows curved up when he asked the question.

"Lectures, ballet, baseball, the zoo, aquariums," Suzanne shot back, like a roller coaster building up steam, ready for the descent. "And flower gardens, arboretums, museums, planetariums, books in real libraries. Rooms full of books, Rudy. And colleges and universities where you can learn to become anything you want."

Rudy was not impressed.

"First of all, we're going to Metropolis Junior High School and Metropolis doesn't have a flower garden or a planetarium or a university," he said. "The second thing is, I'd like to take over my dad's farm after high school. I don't need a room full of books and I don't need to leave Round Knob to become what I want to be."

As far as Rudy could tell, Suzanne's ideas consisted of too much pie-in-the-sky and they were too light on substance to take any sort of root toward becoming reality. It was one thing to indulge in a harmless daydream, but it was quite another matter to use a daydream as a foundation upon which to construct the rest of your life.

World War II was an extremely romantic time. Everyday reality had been temporarily suspended. Whole families had been uprooted, hundreds of thousands of men across America had been sent across an ocean to places they had only heard about or seen in movies.

There had been a concrete, identifiable enemy and the lines of 'good' and 'bad' had been clearly marked. Hellos and goodbyes had taken on an almost mystical quality in the face of such uncertainty.

Suzanne's father had been drafted. Because he was a researcher with Western Union, working out of an old barn in Round Knob, he was one of the first people in the village to go to war. It took exactly six months after he was sent overseas for a bullet to make its way to his brain when he was out in the field. He had been testing a new form of radio communication a mile away from the frontlines.

It had been four years since Suzanne's mother had received the telegram informing her that her husband had been killed. But since Suzanne had been only six years old at the time, she maintained a dreamlike remembrance of it.

She remembered colors first of all – the bright yellow of the telegram. The bold, black letters, "WE REGRET TO INFORM YOU..." The creamy, rouge-colored lipstick her mother had been wearing that morning. The frayed gray of the Western Union employee's uniform who delivered the message. The peculiar paraffin-yellow of the morning sun filtered through an atmosphere washed in an early spring shower.

Next, Suzanne recalled smells – of coffee percolating on the kitchen stove. The light scent of rose water her mother was in the habit of dabbing on the sides of her neck. The smell of bacon frying, sending its aroma across the entire house. The smell of the rain being soaked up by the thirsty earth outside.

There was also the recollection of relatives who flowed through the family home in Round Knob the day of her father's funeral. Aunt Melanie with her high-pitched laugh, especially forced during times of distress. Uncle Ed, with his bushy eyebrows that he raised and lowered compulsively when listening, making a person feel as if they were conversing with a marionette. And ten-year old cousin, Felicity, who had used the occasion to teach Suzanne how to perfectly mimic the sound of a squealing pig.

There were the sensations that Suzanne's brain had chosen to record and retain. It was not a selective process concerned with the event at hand. Rather, she, as a child had a gift to recall the tangential, seemingly insignificant detail and focus tightly on them, even in times of outward confusion.

Often in heated discussions, Rudy would slowly say "focus Suzanne. Focus, will you please?" when it seemed as if Suzanne's mind was meandering off, a thousand miles away from the subject. Actually, it was at these very moments that Suzanne's brain was functioning at its peak.

This sort of mind naturally lent itself to an emotional inclination towards the romantic, which the ever-down-to-earth Rudy could not appreciate. It was not that he was deliberately insensitive to Suzanne, but he was too young to fully appreciate that no two people think alike. He mistook her mental tangents as discourteous behavior meant to change the subject.

Despite the vast difference between them in their personalities, Rudy and Suzanne preferred each other's company over any of their classmates. There was nothing hormonal about their attraction. Fresh air and farm chores kept their bodies in a natural state of balance.

Since every conversation they had was jam-packed with ideas, oftentimes conflicting, it took physical strength to maintain a discussion. Energy that might have been used to fuel the senses was sent directly to their brain cells.

Suzanne and Rudy both enjoyed school and were usually the last to leave after class was dismissed. And so, it was on a November day in 1946 that Rudy Meyers and Suzanne Bazlee and Miss Jane Grunzey were found lingering on the steps of Button Hole School.

The sun was bright and warm in the afternoon sky. Off in the distance a few cumulus clouds, billowy and thick, rode majestically across a horizon of deep blue.

"I'm not so sure that higher education is such a wonderful thing," said Rudy, his eyes focused on the farmland across McDivott Road.

Miss Grunzey laughed. "It's natural to be a little anxious about leaving Button Hole. But you're heading out to something that's better and full of surprises and opportunities for you."

"It's going to be such an adventure!" confirmed Suzanne. "I can feel something happening inside me already. Like my mind is preparing to set sail, just like those clouds out there."

Rudy turned to Suzanne, looking her full in the face. "Yeah, and if you don't watch where your mind is taking you, you'll wind up on the moon with nothing but a pocketful of green cheese."

"What's wrong with green cheese?" asked Suzanne. "Some nice, bright Lincoln-green cheese? That would be utterly amazing. I'd wash it down with scarlet red milk."

Rudy shook his head slowly and smiled.

"Your mind is like a kaleidoscope that takes normal ideas and just completely distorts them," said Rudy. "But I like you anyway."

"Look," Suzanne answered. "There is more to life than Button Hole School or your father's farm or my mother's house, or McDivott Road or Round Knob. Why are you so scared to face that?"

"I'm not scared. I'm being practical."

Miss Grunzey stretched out her arms, getting ready to leave the school house steps.

"You know what I think?" she asked, without waiting for an answer. "I think both of you are right. And I think that you like each other far too much to ever let opinions get in the way of your friendship."

There is something about times of transition that set them apart from the ordinary days in life. Our senses are keen. Awareness is heightened. Our vision is made somehow sharper. Our memory becomes like a sponge during these times. Our very skin soaks in the atmosphere around us.

Of that particular day in November, Rudy would remember when one of the family cows tried to kick him, impatient with his being a bit late for the evening milking, He also recalled feeling unusually sad when he came home to find his father plowing under the earth that had been planted in corn earlier that spring, signaling the end of another harvest season. Graduation from Button Hole School was only a few months away.

Miss Grunzey would recall how natural it had felt to sit outside the school house, talking with two of her favorite students. Her heart would remind her of the pride she felt in their ability and in the ability of all the children she had taught at Button Hole School.

And, true to her nature, Suzanne would remember very little about the actual conversation that took place that day in Round Knob. But years later her mind still retained the image of a red-and-black-checkered sweater Rudy had worn that afternoon, as they sat on the school house steps, with the sweet smell of prairie grass interwoven into the fabric.

Little Mickey Grows Up

There was no getting around the fact that Mickey Michaels was a wisenheimer. A real jokester. A smarty-pants.

It started when he was attending Round Knob School. He was known for encouraging skunks to hang out near the schoolhouse by bringing acorns and other nuts to school and scattering them around the building.

Then he, or one of the other boys, would rile them up, until one would release their "perfume," which seeped through the floorboards. This would usually cancel class for the remainder of the day – or at least cause instruction to take place outside in warmer weather.

Eventually, in 1941, Mickey began attending Metropolis High School, where he was known as "Little Mickey." In homage to his ability to squeeze through small openings, or, if all else failed, pick a lock to gain entrance.

By his senior year Mickey had picked his way through the cafeteria, the gym and the girls' locker room (after hours, of course). In the cafeteria he had absconded with seven chocolate pies. Even creating a special wooden case so he could haul them.

Mickey gained access to the gym for purely altruistic reasons hosting a boys' hour of basketball in the dead of winter, when not much else was going on in town. As for the girls' locker room, despite what you may be thinking, he only went in to post several life-sized photos of his head-shot, with the simple message "For a Good Time, See Me!" hand-written below.

Of course, when confronted by Mrs. Daniels, the school principal, Mickey denied all charges. In the first case (i.e. the missing pies) no one had seen him enter the cafeteria or leave it. In the second case (i.e. the open basketball hour) Mickey had merely used a copy of the custodian's master key, which he had made for such an occasion. Plus, the boys had used the gym for an hour, on a Saturday, when no one else was in the building. And in the third case (i.e. the girls' locker room), Mickey flatly denied that he had anything to do with it, citing the fact that the picture was of him, as purely circumstantial.

"Why would I post pictures of myself," he brazenly asked Principal Daniels. "And leave behind self-incriminating evidence?"

In December of his senior year Pearl Harbor was on everyone's mind. But not so much on Mickey's. He was close to being eighteen. While other male friends began to enlist, Mickey had a different approach. He went with his friends when they signed up, intent on learning what his options were. (In December of 1941, the Selective Training & Service Act was amended. It required that all males, between the ages of 20 to 44 register for possible enlistment in the armed forces).

Although Mickey had two years to go before his 21st birthday, he decided to hedge his bets and enlist in the Navy.

"We're a lot better than the Army, believe me," the recruiter had said. "You join with us; you'll see the world!"

Although it was never the Navy's official slogan, it was enough to convince Mickey who was eighteen and had never been outside of Massac County. Part of the world that Mickey got to see was Normandy Beach. That was because after training at the Naval Academy in Chicago, he was assigned to Newport and came aboard the USS *Augusta*.

Mickey was an Ensign when the USS *Augusta* sailed out of Newport in January 1942. Mickey's ship provided essential anti-aircraft support during the Battle of Casablanca in November of that same year, supporting General George S. Patton. The USS *Augusta* provided the same service in June, 1944, during the Normandy Invasion (D-Day), supporting General Omar Bradley.

By the time the USS *Augusta* was back in Brooklyn's Navy shipyard in 1945, its last wartime assignment (code named "Magic Carpet") was to bring home US service personnel after WWII in Europe had ended in May 1945.

Mickey was honorably discharged at the end of that assignment (December, 1945) having earned the rank of Chief Quartermaster.

By this time, he was the personification of a Navy man who had, indeed, seen the world. Or at least a good chunk of it.

Which begged the question, what was next?

He began seeking the answer by taking advantage of the G.I. Bill (also known as the Serviceman's Readjustment Act of 1944), which included payment of college tuition and living expenses for returning veterans who had served during WWII for at least 90 days and weren't dishonorably discharged. Fortunately for Mickey, WWII had pretty much put the kibosh on his shenanigans. So, for all intents and purposes, he had been a model sailor.

So, when he appeared in the Admissions Office of the University of Illinois at Urbana-Champaign, Mickey had four years' worth of pent-up wise-guy to unload.

"How can I help you?" the admissions officer began.

Mickey, quickly glanced down and noted the name plate on her desk, noting her first name was Susan.

"I'd like to see someone about my application," he began, smiling. "I'm not exactly sure which area of interest to pursue."

"Are you a veteran?" Susan asked, observing that Mickey looked a few years older than the typical just-out-of high school entrant. She also noted he had beautiful brown eyes and thick auburn hair.

"I am."

"What sort of training did you have in the service, sir? Anything applicable to academic or career interests?"

Mickey laughed.

"I was in the Navy and I followed orders. A lot of orders."

Susan was a little flummoxed at the answer. She was a very practical person and it had been a long day. In the months following V-E and V-J Day her office had been inundated with aspiring ex-military collegians. Most of them were just as perplexed about their future as she was.

"How does following orders translate into post-military experience?"

Mickey read the frustration in her blue eyes and decided to back off a little.

"Well, I grew up in Round Knob," offering a bit of personal history.

"I'm sorry, but I've never heard of it," she said, looking up.

"It's near Metropolis. Massac County. Southern tip of our great state."

Susan drew a blank. "I'm from Evanston, just north of Chicago."

Mickey didn't skip a beat. "I spent six months in training at the Naval Station Great Lakes. Went into the city every chance I got."

"I stayed away from sailors."

He raised his eyes is surrender. "We could have crossed paths in the Loop. On Michigan Avenue. Any number of places."

"During the war I was right here. Getting my degree."

"So, you should be pretty familiar with my options then?" Mickey tried to sound hopeful, even if he was feeling a little hostility coming from her. "Look, I'm not asking for a date. I'm just a guy who is trying to get along here. I've seen the world, but I never took formal education too seriously."

Mickey handed his completed application to her. She looked it over.

"You graduated from Metropolis High School, then enlisted? Did you have any jobs while in high school?"

He laughed. "I helped my dad out on the farm. He and my two brothers. We had a small dairy farm and grew crops."

She looked up at Mickey and smiled. *He's not a bad guy, just needs a little focus in his life.*

"And what outside interests did you have?"

"I was a bit of a smarty-pants if you want to know the truth," he began.

She laughed. "How so?" she asked, looking Mickey straight in the eyes.

(Susan was used to veterans' come-ons. But so far, no one had been so up front.)

"Well, there was the time I broke into the band room and polished the brass instruments with linseed oil. The next practice was very interesting."

"You were in the band?"

"I played the bass drum."

"So, you're musically inclined?"

"I'm no Buddy Rich, but yeah. I get by."

"Enough to consider music as a career?"

Mickey laughed. "No ma'am. Not really."

Susan dug a bit deeper into his application.

"You indicated an aptitude for shop class?"

"Well, that's where I learned how to copy the janitor's key."

Susan sighed. "Mr. Michaels, is there anything that you take seriously enough to devote study to it?"

Mickey was pleasantly caught off guard by the question. *At least she's not seeing me as just another in an endless line of veterans knocking on the door of higher education by way of the G.I. Bill.*

"I could have used a little counseling in high school," he admitted. "Actually, the Navy was a spur-of-the-moment decision. But looking back, it was about the best thing that happened to me."

"How so?"

"It taught me responsibility," Mickey paused. "Almost by default. Up until then I had never thought that life had an ending. Or that actions had consequences."

"So, you grew up?" she raised her eyebrows a little.

"Yes. I suppose I did."

After a few minutes of exploring career choices and requisite academic training, Mickey picked counseling. *Of all things, who would have thought that the high school goof-off would be inclined to help guide any kid to anything?*

Mickey left Susan's office and got an appointment with an academic advisor, who helped plan his first year of college at the University of Illinois.

To his surprise, he found his Introduction to Psychology course fascinating. He was amazed that he loved learning. It was as if he was making up for lost time. He found that being allowed to choose the classes and the course of study was liberating. Totally unlike high school or any other academic experience he'd ever had.

While in the Navy, he had taken advantage of the ship's modest library to read every book it contained. At the time, it had been a simple solution to relieve stress and boredom. But unwittingly, he had discovered a voracious intellectual appetite.

Now, as he settled into living off campus in Champaign, Mickey found that he was not nearly the jokester he once was.

Inbetween classes during his second semester, he was in the library studying when he heard a somewhat familiar voice whisper, "Mickey?"

He turned around to find Susan alongside him, smiling.

His eyes turned to an empty seat, inviting her to sit down.

"How's it going?" she asked.

"Good," he smiled back. "Not to brag, but I got a solid 3.5 average first semester. I mean, this sounds corny, but I'm loving this!"

"I'm glad to hear it."

"Your degree is in counseling, right?" he asked.

"Yes. My bachelor's was in psychology. My masters is in academic counseling."

"You went to this school?"

"Yes."

"But, you're from Chicago. So, why in the world would you leave that city and come here? Look at all the choices you had there!" *There's a story there*, he thought.

Susan looked at Mickey and could see he was clearly interested in her life before Champaign and the University.

"Chicago was a great place. But I grew up in Evanston. As a kid, my family would take lots of trips into the city to visit the

Museum of Natural History, the Art Institute, Adler Planetarium and a bunch of other places. But we didn't socialize there."

"You were a museum girl, then?" he smiled.

"I was interested in learning," she explained. "I know next to nothing about shopping the Magnificent Mile."

"Any brothers or sisters?"

"If you want to learn anything more about me, we'll have to do it over lunch sometime, ok?" She pointed to the clock. "I came in here to look at a journal, inbetween appointments. That's one of the perks of working here."

"What about supper?" he casually asked. His heart was uncharacteristically racing.

"Friday? I can meet you at the Italian place on Grossmier. It's not that far from campus."

Susan awkwardly stuck out her hand and he shook it.

During her own time spent as a student, she had pretty much divided her time among classes (which she attended faithfully), the library (she loved its quiet and comfort) and studying (which was just about the only time she felt comfortable in a group).

She wasn't shy, far from it. But she was definitely an introvert. Susan could easily engage in conversation as long as the subject matter wasn't herself. She had no qualms about sitting toward the front of her classes. It was easier for her to understand and read any notes the professors wrote on the chalkboard. If she had a question about the material, she spoke up. She took advantage of professors' office hours whenever she wanted additional insight. But she could not, for the life of her, seem to negotiate the social aspect of college.

Growing up in close proximity to a big city didn't seem to help overcome her DNA. Neither did having a mind that desired to go deep into any subject she chose to explore.

That intellectual curiosity was the hallmark of Susan's childhood. She often laid awake at night pondering what an elementary school teacher had tossed out as an aside. For example, take addition, which led to multiplication. Susan had asked Miss Findley if multiplication ever came to an end.

"Can't you just keep on multiplying a number, forever?"

"I suppose so, Susan," she had said. "Numbers really don't have an end to them."

The rest of the class was too bogged down in memorizing the times tables to care. But Susan's brain almost exploded as she thought about infinity on the way home.

At dinner that evening, when her parents went around the table asking each of their three children how their day went, Susan remarked "Infinity is sort of like eternity, isn't it?"

And that was the exact same question she was pondering over supper at Coscarelli's with Mickey.

"Einstein was absolutely right about relativity, don't you think?" she asked, taking a bite from her lasagna.

Mickey held his forkful of penne in mid-air. "I haven't gotten to physics yet," he said.

"I mean, time is what you make of it. Haven't you spent five minutes with someone who made it feel like forever? Or the reverse? How else can you explain the sensation of time speeding up when you're having fun, or exploring a new idea?" *I'm probably talking too much, but I'm going to go for it,* she thought.

"I'm no expert on the subject, but I think Einstein was talking in scientific terms."

"Which have relational and spiritual consequences!" She was getting excited.

"Well, I agree as far as what time can feel like. The high school clock ticked pretty slowly until senior year. Growing up in Metropolis the fall and winters seemed to be in a separate time zone with nature. Not much was happening, except feeding and milking the cows and feeding the chickens."

"But nature mimics the spiritual dimension. It ebbs and flows, especially when you're paying attention to it."

"Susan, most of my life I took for granted. Until the War." He paused and took a drink of wine. "Metropolis was like the Ohio River to me. Plenty of times my buddies and I went fishing and just looked out for hours from the banks. But our focus was only on a very small part of that gigantic river. And the town I grew up in was an even smaller piece of the pie."

"Evanston's just as small, relative to Chicago" she told him. "Which I guess proves Einstein's point. No one can understand the totality of things."

"Except God." Mickey surprised himself with the quickness of his answer.

"You believe in a supreme being?"

"Sure I do," he took another bite of his dinner. "But now we're crossing over into theology."

"Religion isn't a subject I'm comfortable with." *That's an understatement*, she thought. Susan's childhood had been strong on science, but light on spirituality.

Mickey continued. "I'm not talking about religion. I'm talking about God."

Susan raised her eyebrows. "Is there a difference?"

"Well, I would say religion is human beings trying to make sense of God. But theology is pure God. Without the distractions."

She was intrigued. "What do you mean by 'distractions'?"

"Differences in dogma. For instance, any religion that states its particular creed is the only truth, and everything else isn't. That can't be God. That's human beings arguing over their interpretations of their faith."

Faith? That was another subject that Susan hadn't really thought a lot about. She took her parent's agnostic view as a given. She was encouraged to check out other religions, and she did for a while. Until she found each of them ultimately demanding a commitment to their brand, in one form or another.

Mickey, on the other hand, had questioned his parents' religious beliefs from a young age. The unwritten law in their household was mandatory attendance at a church that preached fire-and-brimstone. Needless to say, Mickey wasn't sold. He was no scholar, but he figured if God created humans, fully knowing what they were capable of, God had to be a lot more lenient and loving than the pastor taught.

"So, I'm curious. What do you believe in?" Mickey asked the question with no trace of judgment.

She put her fork down and looked him in the eye. "Up until the past few years, I really didn't spend much time thinking about faith or beliefs at all," she began. "But the War. What happened to my people in Europe shook me."

"'Your people'?" Mickey was a little confused.

"Both my parents are Jewish. My last name is Finkel. I've got relatives who were lost to the gas chambers."

"I am so sorry." He instinctively reached out and put his hand over Susan's.

"My brother had a very personal reason to enlist in the army. Even before the United States officially entered the War, my parents knew something wasn't right. Family members living in Germany wrote to us about the Kristallnacht. They wrote about coming to work and finding windows defaced with "Juden" written across them. They wrote about the laws regulating what Jews could and couldn't do. They wrote about increasing pressure to leave. And those who didn't came up missing."

Mickey swallowed hard and kept listening.

"My brother was among the troops that liberated Dachau. He's never talked much about it, except to say it was horrible to face what humans were capable of. His experience only reinforced my inclination to not put faith in anyone or anything."

"But what about God?"

"We're not even one generation removed from that horror," Susan said matter-of-factly. "It's too soon to consider what ultimate goodness could look like. That requires way too much faith for me."

"What about love?" he asked.

"What about it?"

"Would you consider the possibility of a loving God who grieves in the face of evil?"

She smiled. "The thing about love is that you have to have faith. You can't really love completely without it."

"So, you're sort of stuck?"

"For the moment." Susan slowly folded her napkin, placing it on the table. "What about you? What gives you such confidence in a loving God?"

"I'm not always confident. I don't have all the answers. But I've learned to trust. Without trust, faith is impossible. And when it comes down to it, my faith isn't based in logic. Just think about love for a second, independent from anything you believe about God. How does love work? How does a person decide to love someone?"

"It's not a conscious choice," she answered. "Everyday moments build up over time and form a bond. That bond breeds trust so the friendship deepens into love."

"It's the same way with God," he said. "We're supposed to be made in God's image."

"Pardon?"

"God gave us free will. We're the only part of creation that can make moral choices. So, we can approach God. Have a relationship with God, if we want it."

"You honestly believe that?" Susan was trying to reconcile her first impression of Mickey the day he was in her office to enroll in classes, with the man sitting across the table from her. "But you were such a wise-guy!"

He laughed. "Shocking, isn't it? I may have grown up a little since V-E Day but I haven't lost my sense of humor."

She leaned a little closer to him, almost whispering. "I'm happy that the War didn't wreck your funny-bone, but you haven't answered my question."

"I believe what I said about God and friendship and love. All of it."

Susan whistled under her breath. "No offense, but when we first met, you didn't strike me as a future philosopher. And then that day in the library? I was watching you before I came over to your table. To see if you were actually keeping your eyes on a book; and not checking out co-eds. I was surprised."

"Hopefully pleasantly?"

She nodded in the affirmative. "You've got to understand. I've done academic counseling for hundreds of veterans. A lot of them are looking for a wife, or a girlfriend. Right now, I'm not interested in that."

Mickey smiled. "Then why are we sitting here?"

She swallowed hard, remembering she was the one who had suggested the idea of meeting over a meal. "That day in the library. You were beginning to get personal, and asking about my family."

Mickey nodded.

"I don't often come across that many guys who express that sort of interest."

"How else are you going to get to know someone?" he asked. "You take a chance and ask questions."

"But your questions are different."

"How so?"

"We've talked about Einstein and God and the Holocaust in the same conversation."

"Isn't it all sort of related?" He smiled.

"Which is why I wanted to have a meal with you."

"Did I pass the test?" he teased.

"Yes," Susan smiled back.

The Barbershop

Matthew Logan's barbershop was located on Ferry Street, right across from the First United Methodist Church.

It was a simple place, with one chair, and three seats for customers waiting for Matthew to give them a haircut.

Because he knew all of his customers, he didn't need to ask them if they wanted just a trim or a haircut. None of them were style-conscious and their primary reason for sticking with Matthew was because his place was one of the few where a person could loiter away some time on purpose.

Being a simple man, he purchased the modest, two-story, red-brick building when it came up for sale and quickly dubbed it "The Barbershop."

When he opened up in the summer of 1950 his first customer had been Presley Hoselmeyer. Presley was a farmer who had taken over his dad's 120 acres when he came back from WWII.

"Morning!" Matthew had begun the conversation easily enough, being the outgoing type, motioning for Presley to take a seat in the barber chair.

Presley nodded.

"What'll it be?"

"Haircut. And short," he answered.

"You do outside work?" Matthew ventured a guess from Presley's weathered face and arms.

"Farming."

"What kind?"

"Mostly corn. Eighty acres of it. And twenty of alfalfa."

"Any livestock?"

Presley laughed. "Only a cow for milk and a few chickens."

"Was that funny?" Matthew reached for his clippers.

"Livestock can be a ball-and-chain. You really can't go any-where off the farm for more than half a day. And these days you'd be hard-pressed to find a neighbor down the road who could spare the time to do your chores."

"I never thought of that."

"That's because you aren't a farmer." Presley paused to take a good look at Matthew in the mirror. "You aren't from around here, are you?"

Metropolis was just big enough that it was possible not to know everyone in it.

Matthew shook his head.

It would take two years of haircuts before Matthew and Presley became acquainted enough to be on the way to becoming friends.

On the other hand, Arnie Adams struck up an instant friendship on his first visit.

Arnie was also a farmer and came into Matthew's shop wearing his overalls.

Arnie smiled as he sat down in the barber's chair. "I don't usually dress up just to go into town. Except for church."

"Your clothes don't look like they've been in the fields yet this morning," Matthew said.

"Well, I milked my cows and fed the chickens, but that's about it."

It was the beginning of spring in Metropolis. Too early to do much of anything.

"Where's your farm?" Matthew asked.

"Near Round Knob. Maybe eight miles away from here, as the crow flies." Arnie paused a moment to take a good look at Matthew. "You have family in town?"

"My folks are from Vienna. It's about twenty miles north of here."

Arnie whistled. "My family's been up to Dixon Springs Park a lot. Beautiful place. And the Diver Down in Golconda has the best blueberry cobbler I've ever tasted."

Matthew laughed. "I've been there. You're absolutely right."

"Of course I'm right," Arnie told him. "I never kid around about dessert."

Arnie proceeded to let Matthew know that he had three grown children. Two boys and a girl. None of them lived in Metropolis anymore.

"That's just the way it seems to be now," Arnie philosophized "You grow up here and pretty much get out. Especially if you grew up on a farm."

He knew what he was talking about. During WWII Arnie and his wife Esther's sons had joined the military. Ethan had enlisted in the Army right before the draft was instituted. Cal had chosen the Navy.

"After the War my boys had the GI Bill and they aimed to take full advantage of it," Arnie explained.

"Ethan went with the University of Illinois and eventually became a geologist out west. Cal settled on Michigan State University and got into banking."

"So, why did you stay then?" Matthew was curious.

Arnie sat up straight, admiring his haircut in the mirror. "Well, I'm half-in, half-out," he smiled. "Esther and I are almost retired. We saved up most of the money she's made working at the Good Luck Glove Factory for a down payment on a smaller home in the southwest. And I've already got a buyer for my land, once we decide to go. It's always been fertile. Given us good crops."

"Where are you thinking of moving?"

"Arkansas," Arnie answered. "We've got a few relatives out there already. We aim to settle near Little Rock."

The couple had chosen Arkansas because one of Esther's sisters had moved there. Freda was two years older. From a young age she had been extremely interested in her mom's holistic solutions to what ailed you. Of course, back then, the number of medicines you could purchase at a general store were slim. As were the options offered by the town doctor. Those who lived on farms, especially, were prone to try natural remedies first.

Freda also inherited a disposition towards the supernatural, which she got from her own mother. This included knowing when a woman was pregnant, and oftentimes, whether the mother-to-be was carrying a boy or a girl. In the days before ultrasounds, this was considered nothing short of miraculous.

Esther didn't share most of her sister's gifts. But she did have an uncanny ability to find water – which in farm country like Metropolis – was a big help. Farms didn't have access to city water. And digging a well was hard work. For these reasons, when wells needed digging, farmers usually sent for Esther.

Arnie was always bragging about her. "When we do decide to head south, there's lots of people who are going to miss her."

"Why's that?"

"For one thing, she's a dowser." Arnie said. "She can detect where water's running underground, using a special stick."

Matthew smiled knowingly. Vienna was much smaller than Metropolis. When he was a young boy growing up, there were less than a thousand people living there.

"My dad and mom ran the general store. So we lived in town. But word gets around, you know. Every farmer sooner or later had a reason to come to our store. You didn't have to ask around much to find someone who could find water on your property."

Arnie nodded in agreement, continuing to brag about his wife. "And she makes the best rhubarb pie!"

Matthew raised his eyebrows. "With strawberries?"

"No. Straight rhubarb and just the right amount of sugar. Her crust absorbs all that juice from the rhubarb and it just melts in your mouth."

"Really?"

Arnie nodded. "She knows exactly how to sweeten up the tartness without taking it away. Most folks never learn how to do that. Esther's crust, that's another story altogether! Flaky and crisp."

"You're making me hungry!" Matthew smiled as he pulled Arnie's smock down to trim the back of his neck. After a minute, he was finished.

"So, what do you think?" he asked Arnie.

Arnie quickly gave his opinion. "Looks good!"

The truth of it was Arnie wasn't too particular. At this point in his life, he combed what was left of his hair straight back.

The sign at Matthew's cash register said "All Haircuts $1.00." Arnie pulled out a dollar from his wallet and a quarter from his pocket for a tip.

Arnie knew full well that Esther was more than capable of cutting his hair. She had done so many times. But then Arnie, being the sociable person that he was, enjoyed going to the barbershop as an excuse to get into town, especially in the winter, when farm chores weren't as demanding.

After Arnie left the shop, Matthew had some downtime. So, he took advantage of the early spring sunshine and stepped outside. He had set up a wicker chair along the sidewalk and sat down, closing his eyes.

"Hello!" Matthew heard the soft, feminine voice before looking up.

It belonged to Valerie Slayton, who owned the flower shop directly across the street. She saw Matthew sit down and walked across the street to introduce herself.

"Good morning!" he smiled.

"Lovely day, isn't it?"

He nodded in agreement.

"Metropolis is wonderful this time of year. Right before the spring planting. The earth is coming alive and the bluebirds are back. It's so hopeful!"

"It is," Matthew nodded.

"I'm Valerie Slayton, I own the flower shop across the street," she pointed for emphasis.

"Matthew Logan," he stuck out his hand. "The new barber in town."

Valerie laughed. "And the only barber! I doubt you'll have much competition."

She had a strong, uplifting laugh. The sort of laugh that gave you hope just to hear it.

Like a lot of folks in Metropolis, she had grown up on a farm just outside town. Her mother had kept flower beds along the south side of the farmhouse. In fact, when company came over during the spring and summer, a tour of what was currently blossoming was always a high point.

As Valerie grew up, she was drawn to the beauty of those flower beds, helping her mom weed and cultivate them. She especially enjoyed helping to make bouquets.

After high school Valerie went to Southern Illinois University in Carbondale, majoring in business. Two months after graduation, she opened up her flower shop, decided to purchase the two-story building, and lived on half of the top floor. Being eminently practical, she rented out the other half to a friend who ran a dance studio.

Valerie's shop had been open two years before Matthew came to town.

"You'd be surprised how many farmers think to order floral arrangements," she said. "And the demographics around here are changing. Since the war more and more folks are moving off the farm."

"Well," Matthew responded. "It seems like you and I have businesses that have pretty good staying power, wouldn't you say?"

"I would," she answered, taking a good look at Matthew before continuing. "You're not from Metropolis, are you?"

He shook his head. "Vienna." (Pronouncing it "VI anna," with the emphasis on the first syllable, the way all locals did).

"It's on the way to Dixon Springs! I love that little town. And the Springs are gorgeous, aren't they? What a lifesaver that place was growing up!"

Mathew raised his eyebrows. "How so?" Truth be told, he already knew of the benefits of cool, running water on a hot day. But he wanted to hear Valerie tell it. Her voice was pleasant and soothing.

"In July and August, weekend trips out to Dixon Springs were such a relief from the heat and humidity. We'd pack a picnic lunch and escape the farm for a day."

"My folks weren't farmers, but we loved the Springs too."

He gestured to the seat beside his. "Please, sit down for a bit."

She gladly accepted his invitation.

"What brought you to our town?" she asked.

"After the war I had a hard time settling down. I went off to Chicago for college. Earned extra money cutting hair. Word spread and it turned into a nice side business. The dad of one of my classmates invited me to have my own chair in his shop, right in the Loop."

"Wow, that must have been exciting!"

"It was pretty heady stuff for a twenty-three-year-old. All sorts of folks came through the door. But after a few years I'd had my fill of the Windy City."

"After college a friend invited me down to St. Louis to work in her florist shop." Valerie said. "I was there a week. Until I heard that the building across the street here was for sale and I jumped at the chance."

Although it wasn't a major piece of information, Valerie had never told anyone outside of her own family, about living in St. Louis. It had been a very short stay. But it had also involved a major life decision that set the course for her life, so far.

The earth had always been a foundation for her. Especially the red clay of the farm where she grew up.

Matthew turned toward the flower shop. "It looks like you've done a good job."

Valerie nodded. "After Chicago, Metropolis must seem like small potatoes."

"It seems like home," he smiled, taking a good look at her green eyes.

In that instant, Valerie decided that she could trust Matthew.

Her high school sweetheart, like almost every other young man in town, had enlisted right after Pearl Harbor. There were tears on both sides when he boarded the train that took him to basic training. He had hugged her close and promised to come back.

It was a promise that the invasion of Normandy and D-Day didn't let him keep.

Valerie had been sitting on the porch of her parent's home that sunny afternoon in mid-June when she noticed Alfie riding his bike up Catherine Street. He was a freshman at Metropolis High School and had a part-time job delivering telegrams for Western Union.

It got to the point that you'd say a silent prayer when you saw him coming up your block.

He was young but intuitive and polite. And that month in 1944 he had gotten some practice in delivering upsetting news.

"Telegram for you Miss Valerie," he began, handing her the yellow envelope. The telegram was addressed to her because her sweetheart had included Valerie along with his parents as those to be notified in case of death.

She knew instantly what it said.

"Would you like me to stay a while?" he asked.

Valerie pressed the telegram to her heart. "No. Thanks just the same, Alfie."

"I'm very sorry," he looked her in the eye. Even if the Western Union office manager hadn't instructed him to offer moral support, Alfie would have done it anyway. It was the least he could do.

Valerie waited until Alife was half-way down the block before unfolding the telegram. "WE REGRET TO INFORM YOU..."

The tears started to flow so fast she couldn't read the rest of the sentence.

Then the thought came, *War is such a ridiculous way of handling conflict. If all the women receiving these telegrams got together, we'd figure out a better solution.*

That fall Valerie had enrolled at Southern Illinois University.

Being a social person, living in a dorm with other women to talk with helped her healing process. By the time of her conversation with Matthew, she'd had five years to gradually let go of the grief she had felt.

And the truth of it was, Valerie wasn't one to give her heart away. In fact, her high school sweetheart was the first and only one who had earned that privilege.

Little did she know that during the war Matthew's company had been one of the last to disembark onto Omaha Beach.

He had to step over the dead bodies of soldiers to advance. The initial shock almost instantly turned to numbness in order to survive.

Afterwards, his mind couldn't come to grips with what had just happened. From where he stood, there was nothing heroic about D-Day. Earning a degree in philosophy from the University of Chicago was as much for his own moral survival as it was anything else. It also helped him re-adjust to coming home.

He wasn't quite as social as Valerie, but he was a person who deeply appreciated the value of friendship. And it was with this appreciation that he listened as she continued their conversation.

"So, it sounds like you've been searching for something?"

Valerie couldn't have known how long Matthew had been seeking. Or where the search had taken him. But she had seen something in his brown eyes. A peace. A settledness. Both of these things stoked her soul to trust him as they sat next to each other outside Matthew's barber shop.

Slowly he formed a big smile. "Yes, I have. Everything I've been looking for is right here."

"Welcome home!" she smiled back.

Artie Gets the Scoop

It was a slow news day. A *very* slow news day.

Artie McCleason sat on the steps of the gazebo in Washington Park.

He was finishing his lunch break, having picked up a sandwich at the Metropolis Diner. It was an unusually balmy November 21, 1963 so he decided to eat outside.

Then he checked in with Liz Hoffmeister who was working the reception desk at City Hall a block-and-a-half away.

"Anything noteworthy today?" he asked, walking up to the open desk on the first-floor lobby where Liz worked the switchboard for lunch-hour relief.

"I've got nothing, Artie."

"Scouts honor?"

"Honestly," she blushed. "This isn't Paducah. If you want to cover a bigger beat, you're going to have to leave Metropolis altogether."

"What? And give up this bustling burg?" he laughed. "At the height of my career?"

Artie had graduated from the University of Illinois in Springfield on the GI Bill. He had enlisted in the U.S. Army right out of Metropolis High School, testing high for an ability to analyze aerial photography. So the Army kept him far away from the front, trying to pinpoint hidden artillery being set up.

He was good at math and could estimate coordinates with uncanny accuracy.

After WWII he had come home filled with ambition. He wanted to cover the news, to be the first one to find out what was happening.

And Artie was good at it. So good that he landed a job with the *Chicago Tribune* covering crime. But he eventually turned cynical and wasn't especially thrilled to be the first one at a murder scene. Then he had a heart-to-heart chat with the City Editor, who re-assigned Artie to local politics.

A year or two into the beat, Artie found he could only stomach the inner workings of the Windy City with a shot or two of scotch. After another couple of years the number of drinks had increased significantly.

This time the City Editor, Max Friedman, was the one to initiate the conversation.

"You wanted to see me, Chief?"

As city editors often do, Max got right to the point.

"Artie, you're one of the best writers I've worked with. I don't know anyone who can churn out the copy and keep the readers' interest like you."

Why is he taking time to compliment me? Artie thought. *When is the steam shovel going to hit?*

"Look. Here's my dilemma," Max continued. "You're turning into a great journalist. But you're also becoming an alcoholic."

Two minutes later Artie had been pink-slipped. Because Max had liked him, he gave Artie a severance of two months' pay.

It was enough to get himself checked into a rehabilitation facility in Chicago and then, stone sober, move back to Metropolis.

He had no problem getting a job with the *Metropolis Sun* where his skills were put to work covering the local government beat.

It wasn't the Big City, but it paid the bills and kept Artie out of trouble.

Artie had known Liz since high school. They were two years apart, so they weren't in each other's social circle then. But they knew each other casually. She had married the high school quarterback and divorced him eight years later. The marriage had been uneventful. A classic story of spouses who had never been very close who grew increasingly apart.

Liz had gone to Southern Illinois University graduating with a degree in business administration. She continued her education on-the-job and eventually became Assistant City Manager. She was bright, empathetic and incredibly determined.

"Liz, I'm only doing my job. You know that."

"So, I'm nothing to you except a news source then?" she teased.

"I wouldn't say that."

"Then what would you say?"

Liz hadn't dated much after her divorce. She had no children but two sisters had given her plenty of nieces and nephews to spoil. She wasn't looking for a white picket fence and kids of her own. She had a house, paid her own bills and loved her independence.

But she had to admit that she looked forward to seeing Artie when he made his daily news rounds.

"I'd say you are one of the smartest people in Metropolis," he told her.

"Now you're flattering me to keep your news source."

"I admire you, Liz. There aren't many women I know who have gotten up the corporate ladder as far as you have. Especially in city government."

She laughed self-consciously. "Like I said, this isn't Paducah."

But Liz was proud of her accomplishments. She loved living in her home town and didn't feel any need to move away.

I'm 45. What do I have to prove? She thought. *I've helped push projects and earned respect from most everyone in this town. I don't mind that it's been behind the scenes.*

She continued the conversation. "So, you've never told me why you left Chicago?"

Artie looked right into Liz's deep brown and compassionate eyes.

Normally he would have evaded the question. Particularly in a small town it didn't always go well to freely share the details of your life. But Artie knew that Liz was well able to hold a trust. The 'news scoops' she shared were never of a personal nature.

"I had a problem covering politics and staying sober in the big city."

Liz kept her gaze on Artie, saying nothing.

"I'm a recovering alcoholic. Been sober the five years I've been here."

The switchboard lit up and Liz held a finger in the air to signal she had to answer it.

"Good afternoon. City Hall. May I help you?"

She paused a moment listening to the caller.

"Just a moment sir. I'll transfer you."

Liz looked up at Artie and smiled.

"This may be your lucky day after all."

"Why's that?"

"That call was from the Medical Center for Federal Prisoners in Springfield, Missouri. The Birdman of Alcatraz just died."

"What's that got to do with our fair city?"

"His body is being buried in Metropolis."

"Why?"

Artie was genuinely shocked, which didn't happen all that often.

The Birdman of Alcatraz (Robert Stroud) was the son of an abusive father, fleeing home when he was 13. After committing murder Stroud was sentenced to a prison in Alaska. After killing a prison guard there he was transferred to Leavenworth Penitentiary. He spent 54 years of his life incarcerated; 42 of those years in solitary confinement. Stroud had a reputation for an uncontrollable temper. Nonetheless he tested for high intelligence. He began his study of birds while serving time at Leavenworth. He gained a worldwide reputation as an ornithologist. Eventually, Stroud was transferred to Alcatraz. When he became sick in 1959, he was transferred to the Medical Center for Federal Prisoners.

"I've told you what you need to know to get started, Artie. The rest any good reporter can find out easily enough."

"Can you at least tell me what department you switched the caller to just now?"

"The City Clerk's Office."

"Thank you!" Artie gave Liz a quick hug and bounded up the stairs to the offices on the second floor.

"You're welcome," Liz called out after him, smiling.

Fishing for news scoops aside, Artie had thought, off and on, about going beyond the superficial work-based friendship he had with Liz.

Over the years that Artie had been covering City Hall, he had seen how dedicated she was to her career. Most often she was the press contact who explained details of upcoming municipal projects around town. It was very clear to him how important she was to local government, as well as serving as the liaison to county and state officials.

They had lots of conversations about work. But none about life outside of the workplace.

Artie knocked on the City Clerk's door. It was always open but his knock helped announce his presence.

Jeter Claybourn gave him a nod. "Come in, Artie."

"So, I just heard that an important visitor is coming to town."

Jeter gave a sigh. Metropolis was a small town. According to the 1960 US Census, 7,300 people lived there. News of any kind traveled fast.

"Do you want to give me three guesses or just tell me?" Artie smiled.

"Seeing how we're only another work day away from the weekend, I'm going to cut to the chase. Besides, you already know the answer."

"I do," Artie shot back. "But that's not the real story."

"What do you mean?"

"It's not so much who died, but why on earth would someone like the Birdman of Alcatraz be buried here?"

Jeter just shook his head. "It really is your lucky day."

"How so?"

"Because the answer to that question is remarkably simple. The Birdman's mother is buried here."

Artie whistled slowly. "Where?"

"Masonic Cemetery. Half-mile north of town."

Jeter scribbled down the phone number to the Medical Center for Federal Prisoners and handed it to Artie. "Anything else you want; you're going to have to dig up on your own."

Artie thanked Jeter before heading back down the stairs to the lobby.

By the time he got to the switchboard Liz had gone out for her own lunch.

So, Artie headed back to the *Metropolis Sun* office where he signaled Peter Wilson, the editor, that he had a scoop.

"Hold the front page!" Artie yelled.

"What do you have?" Wilson looked up from his typewriter.

"The Birdman of Alcatraz just died and he's being buried here in the Masonic Cemetery."

Wilson's eyebrows almost shot to the ceiling. "That's national news. We should be getting an obit from the Associated Press by the end of the day."

"But we'll have the advantage here. The real story is where The Birdman is being laid to rest, and why. And the answer is here."

Artie dialed the number that Jeter had given him. He learned that Robert Stroud's mother, Elizabeth McCartney Stroud, was from Metropolis. She was close to her son and had arranged to have him buried next to her. This was why the Medical Center for Federal Prisoners made the phone call to have Stroud's body shipped to Metropolis after his death.

Artie was in the journalist's version of seventh heaven. He knew he had a local angle that no other newspaper in the country could compete with.

And he continued to contact sources, calling them up by time zones. By nine o'clock he was finished.

"Here you go chief!" he wiped his brow, realizing that he hadn't eaten anything since his lunch time sandwich in the park.

Wilson took the copy and nodded, immediately beginning to read with Artie still standing in front of him.

"Nice work, Artie," he said, finally looking up. "Really nice work! This is tomorrow's front-page lead."

"Just like the big city, huh?" Artie laughed as his stomach growled, causing him to hiccup.

"You're not drinking, are you?" Artie had been up front with Wilson in his job interview years ago, letting him know of his battle with the bottle, and that he had been sober since leaving Chicago.

Artie laughed. "No. I'm hungry, that's all. Scout's honor."

The next morning Artie walked over to City Hall and went directly to Liz's office.

"Thank you!" he grinned.

"For what?"

"For giving me the lead of a lifetime. What are you doing for lunch?"

"Well, if you can go a little late, I have to cover the switchboard again."

"It's a deal! Let's meet at Farley's Cafeteria."

By 12:20 they were both dining together.

"This is a really good article," Liz said, reading a copy of the story that Artie had written.

"It wouldn't have been possible without your help, Liz."

She smiled. "Do you realize that this is the first time we've ever had a meal together?"

"I'm really sorry about that," Artie stopped eating. "It's just that, I've never had really good relationships with women. I mean, never really had time. I wanted to get out of this town so badly after high school. There was a War on. And then college and Chicago."

"Too busy for love?" she teased.

"Too busy for anything but getting the copy written." He paused, feeling awkward having the spotlight thrown on him. "How about you? Why would someone with such potential stay close to home?"

"I love where I grew up. I never really wanted to leave. My parents treasured this town. They were always involved in one way or another. I sort of picked up on their example."

"But you went to Southern Illinois University, right?"

Liz nodded. "Go Salukis!" she said, in reference to the team mascot.

"And you majored in..."

"Business administration. And once I got my degree, I couldn't wait to return home. There was an opening at City Hall and I jumped at the chance. I wanted to be part of improving our city."

"And there's a rule about dating anyone in municipal government?" he asked.

She laughed. "No, but it does make it awkward. Potential conflicts of interest. Besides, you're not the only one who was busy."

Just then, a news announcement came from a radio that was turned on during peak meal hours.

"We interrupt regular programming to give you this special report. President John F. Kennedy was shot in the head, at 12:30 p.m., in Dallas. He was riding in a motorcade and was taken to Parkland Hospital..."

They both put their forks down.

"No!" Liz was the first to speak. "I can't believe it. Who would want to kill such a good man?"

"Every politician has enemies. To get to the national level you've got to step on a lot of toes."

"He's given us so much hope."

"Tell that to his enemies."

They, along with everyone else in the cafeteria that afternoon, sat in stunned silence. After about twenty minutes of what seemed like endless repetition of the events surrounding the shooting, the newscaster paused.

"We've just received confirmation that the doctors at Parkland Hospital were unsuccessful in their attempts to revive President

Kennedy. The President of the United States was declared dead at 1 p.m."

Liz immediately started crying.

"I have to get back to work," she sobbed, standing up.

"Let me walk you back."

It was the longest five-minute walk either one of them had ever taken.

Liz hesitated before continuing up the steps to City Hall.

"This is absolutely horrible."

She stared into Artie's eyes.

He slowly nodded, taking out his handkerchief, wiping away her tears.

All the years of a reporter's accumulated hardness melted away.

Liz opened up her purse, took out a pencil and scrap of paper, and wrote on it.

She had never given her phone number to a man in her adult life. But the afternoon's events accelerated the process of bringing her trust of Artie to another level.

"Here's my phone number," she said, handing him the paper.

"I'll call you tonight," he said, as they wrapped their arms around each other.

Artie stood for a moment in front of City Hall before heading back to his office.

He was half-way down the block before he realized that his story on the Birdman of Alcatraz would never get the national coverage it deserved. As it was, Artie's masterful scoop, severely edited for space, barely made it to page two of the *Metropolis Sun* the next day.

And as he crossed the street, back to the gazebo in Washington Park, a smile slowly came to his face as Artie realized that there was a lot more to life than newsbeats.

Conversations in Farley's Cafeteria

The fact is, most people don't change.

At least that's what Robin Forrest was telling herself as she sat in Farley's Cafeteria eating the Tuesday special.

Robin was sitting in a booth in the far corner. She was waiting for Samantha Conners, a co-worker at City Hall. Samantha was chronically late, but even this was a record for her. Fifteen minutes. For lunch. With no explanation.

"Care for a refill?" Betsy Simons asked. Betsy was co-owner of Farley's, but during the rush she circulated among the diners, offering to top off beverages. "You look like you could use it, hon."

"No thanks," Robin answered.

Betsy put the coffee pot off to the side and sat down. "Hon, you're shaking."

Since Robin was a regular and had worked in the Assessor's Office for six years, they had gotten to know each other. At least as well as any customer and an owner of an establishment choose. (Pleasantries and smiles are exchanged. Along with bits and pieces of information. Some work-related. Some linked to life, in general. Most of it inconsequential.)

"I'm ok." Robin said.

"You sure about that?" Betsy sat down.

"It's Samantha. She works in the Assessor's Office with me."

Betsy nodded. She knew that Betsy and Samantha came to Farley's together at least once a week.

"Something's going on..." Robin paused and shook her head. "Or it could be my imagination."

Samantha had three small children and was married to Kyle Conners. He had worked at a plant that manufactured a form of uranium before it closed in 2017. For more than fifty years the facility had produced uranium hexafluoride, a compound used in nuclear power plants, and in making nuclear weapons.

Kyle had been one of the last supervisors at the plant.

He alerted the plant manager when gas had leaked a few years back. The manager didn't notify the Nuclear Power Commission because the leak was deemed "inconsequential."

But it wasn't to Kyle.

It was the beginning of nightmares he had regularly - to the point that he developed insomnia thinking about what could have happened. It didn't help that he also began to take a second look at some of the customers who used the uranium hexafluoride to develop weapons that far surpassed any 'weapons of mass destruction' of any other country.

So, Kyle became a proponent of non-violence as well as an insomniac.

All of this wouldn't have bothered Samantha so much, except as time went on, her husband became more and more outspoken. This didn't help Samantha's position as assistant to the person in charge of assessing the businesses in Metropolis, including the plant where Kyle worked before it closed.

Over a series of lunches, Samantha poured out her heart to her co-worker.

Their last lunch date a week ago was a doozie. Included in the discussion were Kyle's latest excursions into Paducah – the nearest town that had a peace coalition. At a recent meeting, a guest speaker's topic had been Walter Wink. In particular his book *Jesus and Nonviolence: The Third Way.*

"Ever since he was laid off, Kyle's gotten more and more involved with that Peace Group," Samantha said. "I should have seen it coming. His parents were back-to-the-landers from Bloomington."

"Back-to-the-landers?"

"Hippies," Samantha lifted her arms up in desperation.

"Doesn't that sort of thing skip a generation?" Robin asked, trying to steer the conversation in a positive direction.

"I don't know. Kyle's parents were pretty committed. Enough to leave a university town and set up shop in southern Illinois."

By 'setting up shop,' Samantha was referring to the pottery business Kyle's parents had. It actually earned them a decent living. By trial and error they had learned to make pieces that included the red clay from their small farm.

The Metropolis earth gave their work an aboriginal feel. And it attracted the attention of buyers from Chicago.

As Kyle grew up, he rebelled by studying engineering and eventually got a job working in the nuclear fuel plant. Ethics and morality aside, the work suited him - at least until the shutdown got him rethinking his future.

"Until the shutdown, we never discussed politics or war or anything like that," Samantha said. "I really don't know what's gotten in to him."

"Well," Robin began as they walked through the cafeteria line. "Have you tried listening to him? What's he told you about this Walter Wink guy?"

Samantha's eyebrows arched skyward. "Jesus was a revolution-ary. According to Wink, he was always going around telling under-cover parables that had subtle political points."

"The Sunday school parables?"

Samantha nodded "Yeah. But the way Wink explains it, we didn't understand them the way Jesus' followers did."

"For instance?"

"Like the story about the guy who asks you to pay your debt when you meet him on the street. Back in Jesus' day, it was a way of humiliating the debtor. Because if you couldn't pay, you had to give them your coat. But the way Jesus told the story, the person who owes the money hands over his undergarment as well - which means the guy was out in public, practically naked. And everyone knew the reason why. Absolutely shaming the person trying to col-lect the debt."

"Wow!"

"Yeah, wow. Jesus was encouraging his audience to fight back." As Samantha paid the cashier she continued. "And then there's the story Jesus told about 'if a person asks you to walk a mile, walk two.'"

"What about it?"

"That was in reference to Roman soldiers, who had the author-ity to ask any of the people living within the Roman Empire to do anything. That's one reason why the Jews hated the Romans."

Robin nodded her head in agreement.

"But, to go any further than asked, especially for a Roman soldier, would be extremely unthinkable and also embarrassing," Samantha explained.

"And it would have caused the Roman soldier to admit their own powerlessness in the face of nonviolent rebellion against their empire," Robin added, who was beginning to catch on to the point Wink was making.

"Exactly," said Samantha. "Kyle has been coming home with all sorts of insights. But I don't know what to do with them. Part of me is actually very proud of him. He's growing spiritually. Then part of me is afraid that no one is going to want to hire a junior John the Baptist."

[Truth be told, Robin wasn't much of a church-goer. She had grown up with no particular religion. Her parents had attended First United Methodist of Metropolis, but had never officially joined. They participated in the church's social outreaches, like a weekly soup kitchen, and clothes closet for low-income households.

Robin learned a basic love of others from her parents' example, and the occasional Sunday school lesson that focused on treating others as you would treat yourself. These lessons stuck with Robin into her adult life. Even though she didn't call any particular church home, she had become deeply spiritual.]

"How is the job search going?" Robin asked.

"He's put in a dozen applications for plant safety work within a fifty-mile radius of Metropolis," she answered. "No one who has heard about the plant closing has gotten back to him. I assume they're afraid of Kyle being called in to testify during the class action lawsuit against his former employer."

"Yikes! That really complicates things, doesn't it?"

"Yeah. And he's only got two months' left of unemployment compensation. I mean, we're doing ok right now. It's the future I'm concerned about. Thank God our kids are in high school and we don't have to deal with day care or baby sitters."

As the two friends sat down to eat, Robin picked up the conversation. "Speaking of your kids, how are they doing?"

"It's fifty-fifty. Emily's a senior in high school, so she's mostly focused on getting out of Metropolis and into college. She isn't paying much attention to her dad's spiritual development right now."

"How about Jesse?" Robin was referring to Samantha's youngest, who was a sophomore at Metropolis High School.

"Well, he's the spitting image of his dad, for sure," Samantha began. "He sort of takes after his father in temperament. He's soft spoken and empathetic. And he loves to stick up for the underdog."

Robin smiled. "He sounds like a young man with a caring heart."

Samantha nodded. "But he also agrees with his dad on the non-violence thing. On the one hand, he's such a beautiful kid. On the other, I feel an urge to protect him."

"From what?"

"From people who don't understand that there's more to life than making money. That there are hundreds of ways to measure success other than careers and jobs. In a couple of years, it'll be Jesse's turn to leave the nest and I'm hoping he'll be ready for it."

"Why wouldn't he be? You are such a good mom!"

Samantha shook her head. "Up until this past year, before the plant shut down, I thought I was too. But Kyle has shown me a new side of himself that I didn't know was there. He's been so brave. He's willing to testify against the plant's handling of the nuclear leak. He is so committed to doing the right thing. The moral thing. Regardless of the consequences."

"And that's not a good thing?"

"It could make him unemployable. And we can't be a one-income family."

Robin slowly took a bite of her Swiss steak before responding. "It's going to be ok, Sam."

"How can you say that?" Samantha said. "You don't have any idea what sort of pressure this thing could bring us."

"Your family goes to church on Sundays, right?"

"Yes."

"Then you must believe in God?"

"I do."

"And you believe that God loves you?"

Samantha nodded.

"And that God is for you and your family?"

Samantha nodded again.

"So, shouldn't that help you get through this hump?"

"Hump?" Samantha looked at Robin as if her friend had just grown another set of ears. "This is a mountain range!"

As Robin reached this point in her reminiscing, Samantha crossed the street to Farley's after texting her friend, "Running behind for our lunch date! Will be there in a few minutes!"

"I'm so, so sorry!" Samantha began after she came through Farley's door and went through the cafeteria line.

"Is everything ok?" Robin asked.

[Of the two friends, Samantha had been raised Catholic, but she hadn't been to church in years. She recognized the importance of belief. It was just that, lately, she didn't know exactly what she believed in.]

In response to Robin's question, Samantha shook her head. "I don't need a buffer. I need a belief."

"Can you explain?"

"A lot of people use faith as a buffer. It shields you from life's shocks. Keeps you from falling off the cliff. Like a guardrail," Samantha began to explain. "But that's really not faith. It's an emotional insurance policy. When the you-know-what hits the fan, you take a look at your faith policy and realize you're not covered."

Samantha paused a minute to eat a bit of lunch before continuing. "Actually, now that I think about it, Kyle has much more faith than I do. He's taking a real chance, fully aware of the consequences. And yet he's able to stand strong to his convictions. That takes faith."

"I volunteer at the Bloomington Catholic Worker community once a month," Robin said. "On weekends, I go up there and help with the garden or do other odd jobs. I have friends from college who put me up."

"So, for you, faith is expressed in action? Not by membership in a particular religion?"

Robin sat up straight, looking directly at her friend. "I suppose it's a lot like what James wrote in his Epistle. 'Faith by itself isn't enough. Unless it produces good deeds, it's dead and useless.' But it helps me to understand the difference between faith and religion."

Samantha's eyebrows went up. "Aren't faith and religion the same thing? I mean, they both involve God, right?"

"Well, not to get technical, but Webster's primary definition of faith is tied to allegiance and loyalty. Not belief. Next comes belief in God, and then belief in a religious system."

"But faith requires trust," Samantha replied. "I can't have faith in something or someone without trust - which is probably my main challenge with religion. I can see where faith and religion could be linked, but they are separate. I can believe in God without practicing a particular religion."

Robin smiled. "Yes."

"And I can believe in God and still have doubts about day-to-day life. I'm beginning to realize that I can't grow in faith without help from other people who don't necessarily think the way that I do."

Samantha pushed her napkin to the side of her plate and took out a pen and drew two small dots on it. "Pretend for a moment that this napkin represents all the accumulated understanding of God that we humans currently have. And the two dots represent what you and I know. Then, add everything else that's outside this napkin – this table, this cafeteria, this town, the world, the known universe, and beyond the known universe. Everything else that's outside of the napkin is who God really is."

Robin nodded. "The best thing that organized religion can do is encourage us to love and respect each other."

Slowly it dawned on Samantha that her husband's commitment to social justice and her own commitment to find God were somehow linked.

Samantha smiled as she looked at her friend: "And that's exactly what I'm going to do for Kyle!"

Whitey Farris Opens Up

Comet
Corn Flakes
Milk
Onions
Pasta
Spaghetti Sauce
Ground Beef
Garlic...

Whitey Farris was in the middle of writing down his shopping list on the stenographer's notepad he used for this purpose. The black lines that ran across the light green paper helped keep his words from a downward slant.

Once a month he picked up groceries.

He was concentrating on refilling his pantry when the crunch of a car coming up the dirt road that ran past his house distracted him.

He put down his pencil as the car pulled into the long, horseshoe driveway that led to his front porch.

Soon enough there was a knock and Whitey got up to open the door.

Deacon Patrick's stomach gave a growl, reminding him that he hadn't eaten since six that morning – and it had been nothing but a bowl of cold cereal.

"Good afternoon, Whitey. I would say that I was in the neighborhood, but I know when you live this far out from town, there's no such thing."

Deacon Patrick laughed before continuing. "So, how are you doing?"

Whitey motioned toward the porch steps as he sat down. Deacon Patrick followed his lead.

"You know the saying that time heals all wounds?" Whitey asked.

Deacon Patrick nodded.

"Well, that hasn't been my experience."

Sarie Farris passed away two years ago. She and Whitey had been married for 20 years. The marriage had been a solid one.

Both of them had worked at the Good Luck Glove factory in Metropolis.

He was a maintenance man and she was on final assembly, making sure the glove seams were strong enough to handle a farmer's work.

The Good Luck Glove Company had been one of the major manufacturers of working gloves in the US. Mr. Lurie, the owner, had a reputation for treating his employees with respect and kindness. Holidays were marked by giving hams to each person who worked there.

The company had been good to Metropolis. But in 1974 competition and rising costs resulted in Mr. Lurie having to close the plant. It was the same year that Sarie had been diagnosed with cancer and passed on.

The following two years were a blur for Whitey.

He had gotten by on some savings, canning vegetables from his garden, renting out his land for farming, and living a very frugal life. He mostly did odd jobs for neighboring farmers and only came into town for groceries and haircuts.

"It might help if you went into town a little more often, Whitey."

"I go to town when it's necessary. I guess that's often enough."

"People need other people," Deacon Patrick said.

Before Sarie's passing, the couple had been regulars at St. Rose of Lima's, attending mass every Sunday. Whitey helped out with routine maintenance. Sarie had taught CCD classes on Wednesdays.

"I have better things to do on a Sunday," Whitey said. "I don't have to go to church to find God."

Deacon Patrick smiled. "That's true. But how about giving God a chance for you to find him in other people?"

Whitey slowly shook his head. "What's the point? God's supposed to be omnipresent, right?"

"Sure."

"Then why doesn't God just do us all a favor and show up here? I've been waiting."

"Maybe it's not supposed to work that way."

"What do you mean?"

"Maybe God's trying to get you to expand your horizons away from Karnak."

"This is my home, Deacon."

"It is. But sometimes we need a nudge to let others help us."

"I've been doing fine, considering."

Considering that my heart's been torn out and ploughed under, he thought.

"This isn't the first time we've had this conversation, Whitey."

Whitey just stared straight ahead, so Deacon Patrick kept on.

"I helped with Sarie's funeral service. I know how hard it hit you. But I've been coming here every couple of weeks ever since."

"And I'm grateful." Whitey turned so he was facing Deacon Patrick.

"I'm happy you're thankful. But it just proves my point."

"How so?"

"You need other company."

"I've got neighbors. I say hello to the farmer who rents my land when I see him. Each time I come into town to pick up groceries, I eat out. Once a month I play cards with Grason up the hill."

"Placing an order for a hamburger and fries isn't the same as having a talk with someone. And that's great that you're playing cards, but that doesn't qualify as a relationship now, does it?"

"What am I supposed to do? Put an ad in the *Metropolis Sun* for a girlfriend? Anyway, what kind of a woman would be interested in dating a forty-two-year-old?"

"You're too young to give up."

"I'm trying my best, Deacon. And if God's so omniscient, shouldn't God have figured out that I don't quite know how to get back in the saddle?"

"Maybe God keeps sending me here because I'm part of the solution."

"By nudging me?"

"By encouraging you. Maybe it's time to give Metropolis another try. I know at least three different companies that are looking for full-time maintenance help."

"Hold on." Whitey went inside, got his stenographer's pad and pencil and handed them to Deacon Patrick.

"Would you mind writing them down? With contacts if you have them."

One of the contacts was Massac Memorial Hospital.

The next day Whitey called the human resources department and scheduled an interview.

It was a Thursday afternoon when he was sitting in the waiting room when his name was called.

"Mr. Farris?"

He nodded.

"Please come in."

"I'm Rachel Shevlin, head of human resources. Have a seat."

She extended her hand and Whitey shook it, noting that she had a firm handshake.

Rachel smiled as she sat behind her desk, looking over his employment application.

"You have quite a lot of maintenance experience. Sixteen years at the Good Luck Glove Company and another five at the High School?"

"Yes."

"It's a shame that Good Luck closed down."

Whitey nodded. "It was a good job."

"You've had experience with boiler and ventilation systems?"

"Yes."

"I've checked your references and they gave you outstanding recommendations. Especially Deacon Patrick."

"He's a good friend."

"You've done a lot of volunteer work there to keep the building in order."

"I help out when I can."

"The only outstanding question I have is about the past two years of your work history. Could you talk about that?"

Whitey forced a half smile. "Well, I've been mostly taking care of my property. Doing odd jobs. Helping a neighbor or two with farm machinery."

"So, you're a farmer?"

"No. But my dad was. I know my way around a tractor," Whitey cleared his throat. "The past couple of years have been an adjustment. The same year Good Luck closed my wife was diagnosed with cancer and died."

"I'm sorry for your loss, Mr. Farris."

She has no idea what kind of a loss it was, Whitey thought. *It's felt like my guts have been torn out and I'm still trying to learn how to eat solid food again.*

Whitey nodded. He wasn't used to talking about Sarie and he preferred to keep the emotions he felt for her buried.

"We'll be making a decision by next week. Can I call you to let you know?"

"That would be fine."

On Wednesday of the following week, Whitey was finishing up lunch when his phone rang.

"Mr. Farris, this is Rachel Shevlin from Massac Memorial Hospital. I'm calling to offer you the maintenance position we talked about, if you're still interested."

Whitey swallowed hard. It wasn't that he was nervous about the work. He was nervous about interacting with people again on a regular basis.

Maybe Deacon Patrick is right, he thought. *Maybe it's time to get reconnected to the human race.*

Two weeks later Whitey was eating lunch in the Hospital cafeteria. He was digging into some tacos when Rachel walked up to his table.

"Mr. Harris?"

He looked up and smiled.

"I was going to ask if you wouldn't mind some company, but I don't want to interfere with your digestion."

"No. I mean, sure, it's fine."

She smiled back as she sat down.

"So, how do you like the maintenance department?"

"I like it. It's really easy to enjoy your job when you're working with a good group."

"Makes a big difference, doesn't it?"

Whitey nodded.

Rachel Shevlin was a native of Paducah, where, growing up she was quite the extrovert.

"Were you born in Karnak?" she asked, figuring that was an easy enough question to answer.

"My dad had a farm there. When he passed away, I inherited it."

"But you don't farm yourself?"

"I was the only boy, so as a kid, I did lots of farm chores."

"Grew tired of milking cows?"

"And plowing the fields and trimming the hedgerows and fixing the tractor."

She doesn't want to know if you liked farm work, he thought. *I better change the subject before I put her to sleep.*

"What about you? How did you get to be the head of human resources?"

Rachel laughed. "Actually, I have a degree in philosophy from the University of Kentucky."

"You're a philosopher?"

"No. The plan was to get my bachelor's and then go on to law school. Three or four years in the work force to shore up some funds and then apply. But like the saying goes, 'the best laid plans of mice and men...'"

"Don't amount to a hill of beans sometimes."

She smiled. "I was going to say 'often go afoul' but I like your analogy better."

"Do you enjoy your job?"

"Oh yes! And I know what you're going to ask next."

Whitey raised his eyebrows. "You do?"

"What does philosophy have to do with human resources?"

"The thought did cross my mind."

"A hospital is a great place to study people. First of all, there's the patients. I pop in to patients' rooms and ask how we're treating them. I handle patient complaints. We're not a big enough hospital to have a separate Patient Advocate so I do that. And we have so many different departments: trauma, in-patient, labs, physical therapy, oncology, x-ray, respiratory therapy..."

"And maintenance."

"Right. You've got the whole human condition here."

Whitey looked into Rachel's eyes before asking the next question. "Considering your degree, do you mind if I ask a personal question?"

"Go ahead."

"What's your take on religion? I mean, do you believe in God?"

"I do. I'm Jewish and my family went to Temple Israel in Paducah. My dad was the rabbi there. I still attend."

"Is he still in charge?"

Rachel shook her head. "He passed away when I was eighteen."

"I'm sorry."

"It was a long time ago."

"Do you miss him?"

"Oh yes. He used to push me to ask the deep questions. To go beyond the superficial. That's probably why philosophy appealed to me."

"What do you think happens to you when you die?"

"Well, our congregation is reformed. There is a belief in the end of time, as we know it. That's the Olam-Ha-Ba. And some believe that there will be a bodily resurrection when the Messiah comes. That's called the T'chiyat Ha-metim. But none of it is taught as official doctrine."

"So, what do you believe?" Whitey asked again.

"I believe in the Olam-Ha-Ba and in the T'chiyat Ha-metim. But not for religious reasons."

Whitey raised his eyebrows as Rachel continued.

"Creation should inform us of the creator, right?"

"Makes sense."

"Every living thing contains the seed for its continuance. Nothing in creation simply ceases to exist," Rachel smiled before continuing, "What do you believe, Whitey?"

"I used to think I had it all figured out. My wife and I went to church every week. But since she died, I'm not just sure anymore."

"Death is a shock, isn't it?"

"Yeah. That's one way of putting it."

The conversation was starting to get interesting, but Whitey had to excuse himself to get back to work.

Two weeks later he was in town getting groceries on a Saturday. He had bought himself a pulled pork sandwich, walked over to Washington Park, and was about to enjoy it.

"Hey, Whitey!" Rachel smiled before sitting down. "What you're eating smells delicious!"

"I'm sorry about that."

"Why should you be sorry?"

"Because it's pork."

She laughed. "That's ok. I'm not strictly kosher."

He looked puzzled. "And shouldn't you be in your synagogue about now?"

"I've already gone."

"Oh... well, I've been thinking about our conversation in the cafeteria. About death."

Rachel nodded her head.

"What you said about knowing the creator through what's been created?"

"That was actually the apostle Paul's idea."

"You know about him?"

"Sure. I minored in religious studies in college. Paul wrote half of the New Testament, so it would stand to reason that I'd remember him."

"Then you may know that he wrote that death would get 'swallowed up in victory,'" Whitey said.

"Do you believe that?" Rachel asked.

"I never really gave it a lot of thought, other than believing in it out of habit. But lately, I don't."

"Because of your wife's passing?"

Whitey nodded. "It's easy to believe in something if you don't know any better. But once you've had actual experience, it's another matter entirely."

"It's a good thing to question, Whitey. Our experience influences our belief."

"Seems like it just brings more questions."

"Brennan Manning said 'It's not objective proof of God's existence that we want but the experience of God's presence.'"

"Do you believe that?" he asked.

"Yes, I do. Our souls crave relationship. That's what makes death so hard, don't you think?"

Whitey put down his sandwich and looked at Rachel. All of a sudden, it was like a veil had been lifted off his grief. He began to cry. Slowly at first.

Rachel lightly put her hand on his arm and he let go.

"I'm sorry. This is really embarrassing."

"You don't have to apologize, Whitey."

Then the snot came.

"Good grief!" he tried an awkward apology.

She handed him a tissue.

The two of them sat there for a minute before either spoke.

"Deacon Patrick from St. Rose of Lima's stopped by a couple of weeks ago," he began. "He was reminding me that we need other people. I was sort of giving him a hard time."

"In what way?"

"I told him if God was omniscient, why didn't God just show up at my place?"

Rachel laughed out loud. The kind of laugh that gives you wrinkles around your eyes.

"So, what did Deacon Patrick say to that?"

"He told me that sometimes God shows up in other people. That was after he reminded me that he'd been coming to my place to visit pretty regularly ever since Sarie's funeral."

"It sounds like Deacon Patrick is a good friend, Rachel said.

"Yes, he is. I've been pretty raw with him sometimes. Complaining about things. But he doesn't criticize. He sits there and listens. Even though he doesn't have to."

"Sort of like God?"

Whitey nodded and offered Rachel half of his sandwich.

Life Beyond Big Jim's

"Tabby, where's the avocados? Are you out of them?" Mrs. Crocker was really concerned because she was counting on making fresh guacamole for her bridge club that evening.

"They're right behind the tomatoes," she answered with an ever-present smile. "Let's go find them."

The silver-haired Mrs. Crocker walked alongside Tabby, who, at five foot, two inches, was only a few inches taller.

Once they got to the produce section, they headed to the salad fixings cooler, where the avocados were displayed underneath a huge "FIVE FOR $5" sign.

"Wow, that's quite a bargain!" Mrs. Crocker said.

"We got a nice shipment yesterday," Tabby explained. "And we have red peppers on sale if you're interested."

"Oh, am I ever!" Mrs. Crocker cracked a smile at her fortune. "Thank you."

It was the hundredth customer question of the morning, but Tabby wasn't counting.

She was the Store Manager at Big Jim's supermarket on Fifth Street and she took great satisfaction in providing excellent cus-tomer service.

"You're most welcome," Tabby gave Mrs. Crocker a final smile before heading toward the cereal aisle. She made a note to have the night stock crew do a refill.

At 11:30 she clocked out in the breakroom where she took her lunch sack from the shelf alongside the timeclock.

She had written her name on the sack with a thick magic marker, TABBY! adding a smiley face.

Tabby always took her lunchbreak at 11:30 with Yvette, one of the cashiers. Big Jim's employees had staggered lunches so the store wouldn't be left short-handed.

"Hey Tab!" Yvette greeted her with a smile. "Haven't seen much of you up front today."

"You know how it goes the day before deliveries. Doublechecking paperwork, talking with suppliers."

Tabby took a bite of her chicken salad sandwich and opened up the snack-sized carton of Honey Mustard Pringles she had packed.

"What do those taste like?" Yvette asked.

"Like potato chips that have a bit of Dijon mustard on them I guess," Tabby said. "It's one of the newer flavors."

"I'm partial to the original myself," Yvette said. "Pringles are unique enough on their own, you know?"

Tabby laughed. "I hear you. But last week when Tom was stocking the salty snacks aisle, I couldn't help but notice."

Yvette got her own lunch and sat down, next to Tabby. The lunch break was only twenty minutes at Big Jim's, so the two of them were silent for a while as they concentrated on eating.

It was more than enough time for Tabby's thoughts to center around her childhood...

She had grown up on Metropolis Street, a block away from the Metropolis Public Library and Washington Park.

"You can't get more Metropolis than that!" she had told her future best friend Izzie Overstadt the day they met during recess in junior high school.

"Who wants a double dose of this place?" Izzie had rolled her eyes, having moved with her family down from Carbondale that summer.

"Come on!" Tabby came to her own defense.

But Izzie cut her off. "And that's another thing. No offense, but who in the world names their kid after a house pet?"

Tabby was undeterred. "My full name's Tabitha. It's Aramaic for gazelle!"

"Then you should definitely try out for track this season," Izzie said.

Tabby nodded. "And St. Peter raised a woman named Tabitha from the dead."

Coming from a family of atheists, Izzie's eyes widened at this piece of information. "Can you verify that?"

"You can read about it in the Book of Acts, ninth chapter," Tabby answered. "She was known for her kindness."

A softness came over Izzie's face. "I'm sorry," she blurted out. "I'm giving you a hard time and it's not your fault I'm stuck in this town."

"Why are you stuck?" Tabby asked.

"Because parents make decisions and kids don't have a voice. My dad's a doctor and the medical center here needed a chief of surgery. Meanwhile mom latched on to the dean of admissions position at Massac County Community College."

"And you had to leave your friends?"

"Yeah. And at the rate I make them, I can't afford to lose any."

"Well, Metropolis is a pretty friendly town."

Izzie rolled her eyes. "Sorry. It's an involuntary reaction. So help me, God. Not that I believe in that sort of thing."

"Your family doesn't go to church?"

Izzie shook her head. "My parents don't believe in the supernatural."

"What about you?"

"I sort of inherited their disbelief. But at this point, I'm open to suggestions."

Tabby laughed. "So, you're more of an agnostic than an atheist?"

"I suppose. Do you believe there's a God?"

"I do!" Tabby was definite in her answer.

"Did one of those Book of Acts miracles happen to you?"

"Actually, no. My parents were killed in a car accident when I was three."

Izzie's eyes widened. "Wow."

"I don't remember much about it. But after that my Aunt Margaret and Uncle Henry took me in. They couldn't have kids, so I became like a daughter to them. They went to First United Methodist and took me with them. I grew up in that church."

"But why do you believe? I mean, it's fine if your aunt and uncle have that connection, but what about you?" Izzie was genuinely interested.

"All those Sunday school lessons started to sink in I guess," she smiled...

All of a sudden Tabby was brought back into the present moment, there in the breakroom with Yvette.

"I gotta scoot," Yvette said, finishing up her soda. "I'm trading ten minutes of lunch for leaving ten minutes early today, remember? Jimmy's got a baseball game and I promised him I'd be there."

Yvette was a single mom and Tabby was supportive of her efforts to be involved in her teen-aged son's life. Yvette's husband had been laid off from his production-line job three years ago. Then he laid himself off from being a father and husband. It left Yvette unmoored for a while, but she bounced back. She was working at Big Jim's full-time while enrolled in Massac Community College's Paralegal program. She and her son had moved in with her mother to help make ends meet. Shortly after that her widowed mom offered to babysit the three evenings a week that classes were held.

"You're a lifesaver!" Yvette had told her.

"Actually, God is honey, but thank you!"

As soon as Yvette left the breakroom, Tabby found herself thinking back again to Izzie. Only this time, they were seniors at Metropolis High School, sitting outside on the lawn in front of the school. It was 1996...

They were taking advantage of springtime, which came early in southern Illinois. It was late April and the violets were already out in abundance. It was a balmy seventy degrees out. Perfect weather for having a conversation.

"I know exactly what I'm going to do after high school," Izzie began. "University of Chicago, here we come!"

"I'm going to Massac Community College, right here in town, and then transfer to University of Illinois at Carbondale," Tabby offered. "I can get a good education, not spend so much on tuition, and work part-time. I don't want to put my aunt and uncle out."

"First of all, you got a scholarship, just like me," Izzie countered. "Second, your aunt and uncle own Big Jim's and you are their kid. Everyone in this town gets their groceries there. They have no problem with money."

"It's not a question of money," Tabby countered. "I don't need to go to a big-name university. That's all."

Izzie looked hard at her friend before continuing. "You and I have been friends forever. The pupils in your eyes are dilated which means you're hiding something."

Tabby smiled. "The only thing I'm hiding from you is how much I love this town. I truly believe that God has me exactly where he wants me."

"Still waiting for your Book of Acts moment, huh? What is it with you and religion?"

Despite numerous conversations on the very same front lawn of Metropolis High School, Tabby had not been able to gain much influence over her friend. *I wish I could just bypass Izzie's brain for one moment*, she thought. *I'd speak directly to her heart. Then she'd understand.*

"I've already had my Book of Acts encounter," Tabby said.

Izzie shook her head. "No. You haven't, Tab. And if you think you're ever going to convince me that a benevolent God held your hand while he took the life of your parents, it's not going to happen."

"But he did. He gave me my aunt and uncle, who have been nothing but kind to me."

"You got lucky. Very lucky. That's all," Izzie protested. "Because of my parents I've been stuck in this one-horse town since grade school. And I'm counting the months until I get to Chicago."

"You have a fine mind. And you've used it," Tabby said.

Izzie nodded. "I'm going to be in the extra-credit hall of fame."

Tabby laughed. "But where do you think all that drive came from? It's not just your DNA, Izzie."

"Sure, there are cultural influences at work too. Hence the drive to get out of this place."

"It's God who's behind it. But you can't see it."

Izzie's eyes formed slits. "You can't see something that isn't there."

"There's so much more to life than what we can see," Tabby countered. "Please don't limit yourself."

Two months after their conversation, Izzie and Tabby walked across the stage receiving their diploma from Metropolis High School. True to her word, Izzie left for Chicago late that summer. She enrolled at the University of Chicago, moved into an apartment with another classmate, and began waitressing in a nearby restaurant. Also true to her word, Tabby stayed in Metropolis and signed up for classes at Massac County Community College. She also worked, part-time at Big Jim's.

At first the two friends kept their promise of staying in touch. Then when cell phones gradually made the concept of long-distance obsolete, they switched to calling each other frequently.

Tabby remembered one recent call, in particular.

"Hey Tab, guess what just happened!"

It was shortly after Izzie had earned her Master's Degree in Artistic Management.

"You know I'm a terrible guesser!"

"Come on, give it a shot!"

"You've been elected Mayor of Chicago?"

"Yuck! Have another go."

Tabby shook her head. "You're doing stand-up? You always had a flair for comedy."

Now it was Izzie's turn to do a head shake. "It's better than that. I'm the new Production Manager at the Chicago Shakespeare Theater!"

Tabby was all smiles. "Wow, Izzie! That's spectacular!"

"Just found out this morning and you're the first person I called. Now you'll have a reason to visit the Windy City more often."

"Keep me posted on the theater's schedule."

"Now that my bit of news is out, how are you doing?"

"Well, Aunt Margaret and Uncle Henry promoted me to Store Manager at Big Jim's."

"That's great, Tab. Now you can finally put your business degree to good use."

"Oh, I have been," Tabby said. "My aunt and uncle are semi-retired now. And they've been prepping me to take over the store soon."

"You aren't just doing this to help them out, are you?"

"Big Jim's is doing better than ever. They've made a comfortable living and now they want to pass along the store to me."

"You're excited about it, aren't you?"

"Yes, I am!" Tabby answered. "We've got eight different sections in the store now. And forty employees. We're still the only supermarket in Metropolis."

"Looks like you've decided to stay put in the Land of Superman?"

Tabby smiled. "Yes."

"Any significant relationships? Is that one of your new departments at Big Jim's?" Izzie teased.

Tabby laughed. "We have a management team at the store now. All the section managers are on it. I'm friends with them and the local farmers we purchase from."

"What about romance?"

"I'm all for it," Tabby answered. "It just hasn't happened yet. How about you?"

"I work with great people. I just don't want to date them."

Tabby decided to switch the subject, ever not-so-subtly. "How's your soul doing these days?"

"I've started going to this little storefront Hispanic church in my neighborhood."

"Do you speak Spanish?"

"No, but I love it. The families there are so welcoming. A couple of members do translation for non-Spanish speakers. They sit in the back and have rigged up a microphone and Headsets so you can hear the translation without interrupting the flow of the service."

"Wow!"

"The pastor is a former professional wrestler. He was on the verge of going national. You know, the WWE. But he felt a nudge to get into ministry." Izzie paused a moment. "I've never been around people who got so excited about God before. Except you."

"That's great!"

"As soon as someone states a need, people in the congregation step up to meet it. You want to know something else?"

"Sure."

"A group from the church hands out groceries each week to neighborhood families. They've gotten together to pick up trash and encourage others to take care of their street. I'm part of that group."

"Izzie, it sounds like you're really becoming involved."

"I'm not an official member, but I like their openness. Want to know the weird thing about it?"

"What's that?"

"They don't preach or hand out Bible tracts."...

Tabby was roused from the pleasant memory of the phone conversation as Yvette came back into the breakroom and sat down next to her.

"Your Aunt Margaret wants to speak with you. She's on the office phone, line two."

Tabby walked as fast as she could up to her office. *What in the world could possibly be going on?* She wondered. She knew that her aunt and uncle would never call her at work, unless it was an emergency.

Tabby picked up the phone. "Aunt Elizabeth?"

There was a deep sigh that came through the receiver. "Tabby, it's Uncle Henry. Earlier this morning, he said his chest hurt and his right arm was numb. I called an ambulance. He's being checked out in the Emergency Room at Massac Memorial Hospital right now."

"I'll be right there." Tabby told Yvette where she was going and headed to the hospital.

Aunt Elizabeth smiled weakly at her as she stood up to receive a hug from Tabby in the ER waiting room.

"Has Uncle Henry been examined yet?"

As soon as she asked the question, over the loudspeaker they heard: "Code Red to the ER. Code Red to the ER."

Aunt Elizabeth and Tabby sat down and held each other tightly.

Eventually, Dr. Kilmer, the on-call cardiologist, came through the doors leading to the ER treatment rooms. He stopped at the desk to ask the ER clerk if family members were in the room, and then motioned for Aunt Elizabeth and Tabby to follow him to a private area, just a few yards away.

"I'm sorry to have to tell you," he said, looking directly at Aunt Elizabeth. "Your husband went into cardiac arrest and we couldn't revive him. He suffered a massive heart attack."

"He had a history of heart problems," she said matter-of-factly, as tears began to form in her eyes.

Tabby held her aunt and gently rubbed her back. "I'm so very sorry, Aunt Elizabeth."

Uncle Henry and Aunt Elizabeth were both very practical people, so the funeral arrangements had been made years ago. They included the service at First United Methodist.

The pastor talked about Uncle Henry's love of his niece. His love of community, evidenced by regular donations to the town's food pantry. He had sent boxes of groceries to families he knew were struggling. For many Metropolis teens, Big Jim's had been their first employer.

The luncheon after the funeral was more like a community potluck. The fellowship hall was packed. Tabby and Elizabeth were sitting next to each other, at a table reserved for immediate family and special friends.

"Well, the store's yours now, Tabby," Aunt Elizabeth smiled and held her niece's hand. "It'll be official once Henry's will is read, but it's not something we didn't already discuss with you."

Tabby nodded. "You and Uncle Henry have taught me so much," she said.

"Oh, I think you've always had a knack for business."

"I don't mean just about Big Jim's," Tabby looked at her aunt. "I mean about life."

Yvette was sitting on the other side of Tabby and tapped her on the shoulder. "I am so sorry, Tabby. Your uncle was a wonderful man. The times he came into the store, he was always in a good mood. He always was giving me tips. Talking about the difference between a good and a great employee."

Tabby smiled. "That sounds like Uncle Henry."

"He noticed the little things. Like if a produce sign should be a little higher so people could easily read it. Or how to arrange the weekly ads along the front window. And he was the one who arranged to have copies of the *Metropolis Planet* delivered to the store so people who couldn't afford the paper would have a chance to see the ads in the first place."

"He really loved Big Jim's," Tabby said. "And the families who shopped there."

"So do you, Tabby. And all of us who work there too. If it hadn't been for you, I wouldn't have been able to go to college in the evenings. Your flexibility in the work schedule is a true blessing."

"It's nothing," Tabby said.

Yvette shook her head and held Tabby's hand. "It is something, Tabby. A huge something. I'm a better mom because of you."

Tabby felt a gentle tap on her shoulder. "Hey, stranger," Izzie said. "Mind if I pull up a chair?"

As soon as Izzie sat down, the two friends held each other.

"I am so sorry," Izzie began. "So very, very sorry."

Tabby continued to hold on to her friend.

Izzie whispered, " 'Precious in the sight of the Lord is the death of his saints.' "

Tabby's eyes opened wide. "Pardon?"

"Valioso a los ojos del señor es la muerte de sus santos," Izzie repeated. "It's from Psalm 116."

"You know Spanish?"

"Just a little. I've attended a few funeral services for friends at church."

"That's great! I mean, it's wonderful that you've kept on attending the Spanish church, Izzie."

"It is, Tab. And I'm not sure that I would have even gone in the first place if it hadn't been for you."

"What you mean? I haven't had much of an influence on you at all when it comes to faith."

Izzie smiled. "Not at first. But then we began to hang out. And I saw how you treated your aunt and uncle, and me. You never had a bad word to say about anyone. I was pretty arrogant on the outside, but I was watching."

And for the first time Izzie allowed herself the freedom to cry in front of her friend.

Friends at a Funeral

Fiona scooped up some of the potato salad from the buffet table and sighed.

She was there for the funeral of her mother, Margaret, and was hoping against hope that she could maintain a semblance of composure until the after-service meal was done with.

She hadn't been back to Metropolis in ages. Twenty years to be exact.

As she made a turn toward the tables to sit down, she had to swerve to avoid hitting McKenzie Field head on.

"So sorry!" McKenzie smiled. Then she did a double-take. "Fiona, is that you?"

Fiona nodded.

"Goodness! Time has been gracious to you, in spades." She backtracked a bit. "I am so very sorry about your mom. She was such a free spirit, wasn't she?"

If that's what you want to call it, Fiona thought. *She was ever the extrovert and you always caught her in a crowd.*

"Are you sitting with someone?" McKenzie asked. "A couple of us from the Class of '92 are here. We'd love to have you join us."

McKenzie nodded toward a table off to the side and Fiona followed.

"Hey Amari," McKenzie began. "It's Fiona Sensoli!"

"Sorry for your loss," Amari said. In high school McKenzie and Amari had been best friends. They had remained close, with both of them still living near Metropolis. Fiona, on the other hand, had left town a week after graduation.

"I can't imagine what you must be going through," McKenzie said.

No, you really can't, Fiona thought. *I'm not even sure where to begin.*

"What have you been up to?" Amari asked. "You sort of vanished."

"I moved in with my aunt in Paducah for a while. Got a scholarship to Southern Illinois University, majored in English. What about you?"

"After high school I got a job working in the Massac County Parks & Recreation Department. I'm a supervisor now."

"And I got access to a trust fund that my dad set up when I turned 21. I learned how to invest and basically live off the dividends." McKenzie had a huge smile on her face when she mentioned this. "I have a house in the suburbs with two teen-aged kids." She paused a moment before continuing. "Divorced. What are you going to do? Right?"

"Did you marry Hadley Brighton? You guys were king and queen of the prom."

"I did, but when I found out he was skimming off the top of my investment portfolio, I dumped him pretty quickly."

Amari piped in. "Hadley has a degree in asset management from Purdue. But he would have been behind bars if McKenzie had decided to prosecute."

McKenzie shrugged her shoulders. "I don't believe in holding grudges. Where does it get you?" She gently nudged Fiona before continuing. "But you haven't told us, where did you disappear to after high school?"

"I didn't want to stay here. That was about the only thing I knew for certain. Graduation night I came home to find my dad and mom had been drinking, again."

"I had no idea." McKenzie was shocked.

"No one knew. They were social drinkers at first, but then it turned into alcoholism. Missed work days. Bills overdue. Yelling and screaming. The night of my graduation they were going at each other something fierce. They were so out of it that they didn't notice when I packed some clothes and took off in my car."

"Wow."

"I stayed with my Aunt Jean that summer. She helped me follow up on my college application."

"That must have been tough," Amari said. "I mean, you were only a teenager."

"I was old enough to realize that I needed to get out if I was ever going to make it in this life."

"What then?" McKenzie re-entered the conversation. "Short of the divorce, my life hasn't been nearly as traumatic as yours." She touched Fiona lightly on the shoulder. "Cash can be a really good buffer."

"College was great," Fiona answered "The professors were good. I made some good friends. I was fortunate to get a job with the Springfield *State Journal-Register* covering state government."

"What fun!" Amari said. "I mean, you were always a creative person. I bet newspaper work fit you!"

Fiona smiled. "It was fun. And I got to work on some really important pieces. But then came the cuts after people stopped depending on newsprint."

She chose not to mention what it felt like to work in an eviscerated editorial department. Where a staff of 25 reporters working various beats had been whittled down to 15, then 10. Only the strongest souls stayed on board. The others, like Fiona, saw the writing on the wall and left before they were pink-slipped.

"Are you still there?" Amari prodded.

"I moved into public relations work for a while. Started a blog. Wrote a couple of books."

"Wow! You're a published author?" McKenzie asked the follow-up.

"The first one was self-published. Then I got an agent and brokered a deal for a second."

"What's your subject matter?" Amari asked.

Should I tell them the truth? She thought. *I went to high school with them, but, on the other hand, what have I got to lose? I'm tired of playing it safe.*

Fiona looked at each of them before answering: "Religion and faith."

McKenzie laughed. "I'm sorry. But why on earth would you pick religion?"

"If we don't choose a religion, it chooses us." Fiona said.

"What do you mean?"

"I worked in the news industry for two decades. For most of that time I covered state politics. If I learned one thing it was that we're all born to worship something."

"Really?" McKenzie said. "I haven't walked into a church since my divorce was finalized. And I don't encourage my kids to chase after angels."

"That's not what I'm talking about."

"Then help me understand."

"Some of us worship success. We chase after position and salary. Some of us worship accolades, we chase after awards and honors. Some of us worship intelligence and chase after degrees and academic recognition."

"What's wrong with that?"

"Nothing's wrong with those things, but on their own, they can be pretty vacuous."

"And organized religion isn't?" McKenzie laughed.

"I'm not talking about organized religion. I'm talking about genuine connection with your spiritual self."

"Fiona, you sound like you've converted to the New Age." Amari wagged her finger in mock protest. "What would your mom say?"

"Mom was the reason we kept going to Mass," Fiona explained. "She was religious. But she wasn't really a spiritual person."

"How do you mean?" Amari asked.

"Being religious means adhering to a set of denominational rules. You're focused on being a Catholic, or a Protestant, or a Jew or a Buddhist or a Muslim or a Hindi or whatever it is you believe in. But being spiritual means you're focused on your spirit."

"Can't you be both?" McKenzie found herself re-entering the conversation.

"Yes. But's it's one of the hardest things for humans to do. The temptation to turn your religious preference into a prejudice is strong. Particularly among fundamentalist types who are so adamant that they know the way to the exclusion of everyone else."

"Which is why I don't push religion on my kids," McKenzie said.

"But your kids have a spirit. That's the crux of it. So often we allow negative experiences with a religion to stunt our spiritual growth. We encounter a doctrinal wall when we're searching for love."

Amari sat upright. "I am so tired of having to put on a happy face every Sunday. It doesn't seem real."

"It doesn't seem real because it isn't," Fiona said. "We're all broken people. Each one of us. Our spiritual ancestors got kicked out of the Garden and we've been searching for acceptance ever since."

"Which gets back to my point," McKenzie interjected. "You'd think that the major religions would have figured that out by now. When will they learn that judging people never works?"

"Maybe it's easier for religious leaders to keep trying to tell us who God is, instead of showing us God by walking alongside us in our brokenness."

"Really?" Amari asked.

"My Mom passed away a week ago. The priest tried to console me by quoting scripture. He wasn't trying to comfort me as much as avoid his own uncertainty with death. It's not his fault. That's what he was trained to do. Offer an institutionalized response to a very personal emotional experience."

"I'm sorry," McKenzie said.

"For what?" Fiona asked.

"For not recognizing how hurt you feel."

"It's ok. You're dealing with your own brokenness. Divorce is a sort of death, isn't it?"

"On one level, I suppose."

"You were in a committed relationship with your husband and now you're not. Because he violated your trust."

"At the time it was such a relief to get the divorce over with. I meant it when I said I don't look back. What's the point?"

"We can't be healed from the past if we ignore it."

"Our whole culture is driven by emotion," Amari jumped in.

"Follow your heart. What does that mean? If I followed my heart I'd quit my job, leave my husband and daughter and max out my credit cards on a nice vacation. I haven't followed my heart in years."

Fiona shook her head. "I'm not talking about letting your emotions lead you around by the nose. I'm saying to face them so we don't join a religion for the wrong reason."

"What would be a wrong reason?" Amari asked.

"Fear. The Bible talks a lot about not being afraid. That God's perfect love casts out fear. But there are too many churches that preach an entirely different view. In those churches you're taught to fear thinking outside of their doctrinal box."

"Then a person keeps going to church out of habit instead of commitment?"

"That can be one consequence," Fiona answered. "Fear also keeps a person from using their brain. Faith without reason often turns into narrow-minded belief."

"Which is exactly why I quit going to church!" McKenzie said. "I'll give you points for mentioning that there could be something to taking a trip down memory lane for a bit. To see if there's anything lingering in my soul towards my ex."

"You were soulmates," Amari said. "It was such a tragedy when you split up."

"But I am through with church. I see no benefit to it."

"What about you?" McKenzie turned toward Fiona. "You haven't said what you believe."

"I'm still trying to figure it out. It's not an easy process."

"We're not letting you off the hook," Amari said. "Give us some details. Are you attending a church?"

"I did. For twenty years. But then I started to question the dogma behind it. And the parish priest wasn't too sympathetic."

"What sorts of questions did you have?" McKenzie asked.

"Why is tradition followed without viable benefit? Like priests can't marry because of tradition. And the infallibility of the Pope. And nuns being treated as second-class citizens. Or no Biblical basis for Purgatory. Or praying for the dead."

"But if the traditions challenged you, why did you stay for two decades?" Amari follow-up.

"Because of the good stuff," Fiona sighed. "Like the peace and social justice teachings within the Catholic church. It's incredible. Leaving was one of the most difficult decisions I ever made. I didn't leave angry as much as disappointed."

McKenzie took a final bite of her sandwich before asking: "Where do you think your mother is right now?"

"Pardon?"

"Do you believe your mom's in heaven?"

"It doesn't matter."

McKenzie raised her eyebrows. "You better be careful. We're having this conversation in the Saint Rose of Lima parish hall!" She pointed to the devotional painting of St. Rose on the wall behind them.

"She was the first saint from the Americas canonized by the Catholic Church," Fiona said, matter-of-factly. "Rose was a Third-Order Dominican."

"Don't avoid the subject," Amari frowned. "Do you think your mom's in heaven?"

"You're asking the wrong question," she laughed.

"Doesn't it matter that your mom lived a moral life?" McKenzie stepped in to defend Fiona's mom.

"Fiona smiled. "Now that's the right question!"

"So, what's your answer?"

"I don't know. Mom had challenges. She lived with an alcoholic husband who influenced her to become an alcoholic with him. It was complicated. I remember my mom being a really kind, nurturing person when I was young. But later on, once the drinking took over, not so much."

"I'm sorry," Amari said, placing her hand on Fiona's.

"I'm sorry too," Fiona said. "I guess it goes to show the power of free will."

"It does?"

"Sure. Fundamentalists will tell you that we sin because God's given us free will. They say we have to make a decision to follow their form of religious practice by using our free will. But if you don't agree with them, then you're pretty much going to hell. So actually, as far as they're concerned, you have no free will at all."

"Your mom went to hell then?" McKenzie asked. "Maybe I'm headed there too because I divorced my husband."

"I don't know where my mom is," Fiona answered. "It's not my business to judge her. But I can learn from her."

"What did you learn?" McKenzie leaned in.

"For openers, it's not as complicated as we make it. Micah got it right."

"Who's Micah?"

"He was a minor prophet. Wrote a book that's included in the Old Testament. He quoted God as saying that true religion was doing justice, loving mercy and walking humbly before God."

"Wow."

"A really easy thing to remember. But not so easy to live it out in real time." Fiona pushed her food to the side. "Sometimes religion makes it pretty difficult to do those things."

McKenzie raised her hands in the air. "And that's why I keep telling you guys, I'm done with it!"

"But giving up isn't the answer," Fiona said.

"Explain yourself!" Amari re-entered the conversation.

"If God created us, then God knows us, right?"

Amari and McKenzie both nodded in the affirmative.

"Then it should follow that God should know what's best for us, right?"

Again, they both nodded.

"And religion is a way for God to speak to us. But we need to be a clean vessel for our soul to hear."

McKenzie paused for a moment. "So, rather than giving up on religion entirely, I should keep seeking?"

"Well, Jesus said, knock, ask and seek, and the door would be open. As long as we're honest and consistent about it," Fiona continued, "We are responsible for our souls. No religion can save us."

Amari shook her head. "Just when I think I understand where you're going with this, you say something that astonishes me. My dad and mom never argued about faith. They were both Methodists. Came from similar backgrounds. Growing up was pretty simple. We went to church as a family until we kids left home. My sister and I never questioned it." She paused a moment and smiled. "Even now my husband and I still go. Every Sunday. Even though I'm not exactly happy about it."

"You mentioned that before," Fiona said. "What's making you unhappy?"

"I'm not."

"You're not what?" Fiona raised an eyebrow.

"Unhappy. It's more like an absence of anything rather than a feeling of something."

"But shouldn't church make you feel something?"

"I wouldn't know," Amari fought back tears. "Growing up we didn't talk about how it feels to be in church over Sunday afternoon dinner."

"Why not?" McKenzie asked.

"Because in my home, we just didn't do that."

"And now?"

"And now I'm raising a ten-year-old daughter and I'm scared to death that the minute she turns twelve, she's going to bombard me with all these questions that I'm not prepared to answer, because I wasn't allowed to ask them."

Fiona leaned forward. "Amari, it's ok to say you don't know. Your daughter's world won't end."

"But mine might." Amari began to cry.

McKenzie handed her a tissue. "Who needs the aggravation? The irony of having to be God's answer man to your kids when you yourself don't know?"

"I feel guilty for not knowing," Amari said, in between sobs. "Shouldn't I have figured this all out ages ago? Not to mention crying at the funeral of your long-lost friend's mom for the wrong reason."

"I'm fine with you crying," Fiona said. "A funeral is a natural time for your soul to want to express itself."

"Thank you," Amari said.

"For what?"

"For listening to me. For allowing me to speak my mind."

"Without doubt there wouldn't be any faith, would there?" Fiona looked straight at Amari.

Amari's mind went back to a time when she was seven. She was with her Aunt Bessy, in the kitchen, helping her make hot-cross buns. Up to that time Amari had wonderful memories of spending time baking with her.

But this wasn't one of those times.

Amari was mixing up the icing when Bessy turned to her and asked: "So what have you been learning in Sunday School?"

"We've been talking about making our faith personal."

"And what does that mean?"

"Starting to understand what you believe."

"I see," Bessy smiled.

"But I don't."

"Why is that?"

"Because I'm not sure that I accept everything I'm being taught."

"Pardon me?" Bessy's eyes narrowed and her eyebrows lifted in disapproval.

Amari looked directly at her aunt. "I'm not sure we're all on the same page in Sunday School."

"What do you mean 'the same page'?"

Amari felt her face flush. Up to that time she had been freely able to speak her mind with Aunt Bessy. But then, she was hit with the reality that certain subjects might be off limits.

"Never mind," Amari had said. "I didn't mean to upset you."

Aunt Bessy tried to backtrack, but it didn't work. It was clear that she felt threatened at her young niece's observation.

From then on Amari decided it would be best to keep her doubts to herself.

McKenzie drew them back into the conversation. "So, having doubts is a good thing?"

"It can be," Fiona said.

"Then why didn't we get that message during religion class? Or were we all absent when they taught that particular lesson?"

"It goes back to the basics," Fiona suggested. "Remember what Micah had to say about true religion?"

"Do mercy, love justice, walk humbly before God?" McKenzie was surprised at how quickly she gave the answer.

Fiona smiled. "As far as I can tell, having doubts is not a disqualifier from believing in God. Or seeking to live a life that would please God."

"So, we don't have to be God's answer-man after all?" McKenzie laughed.

Fiona slowly shook her head 'no.'

"What a relief!" Amari laughed.

Saint Rose of Lima to the Rescue

Patterson walked out of Harrah's Metropolis casino, walking fast up Market Street, taking a right onto East Third.

He was headed to St. Rose of Lima Catholic Church. He just gave away a sizeable portion of his savings account in two days' worth of playing table games.

The plan was to build it up, not squander it.

By the time Patterson opened the front door of the church, he was livid. Mostly at himself. But there was enough anger spilling over to include Harrah's, his family, and the Metropolis Chamber of Commerce.

Patterson sighed as he sat down in a chair at the very front of the church, past the rows of pews. He was staring straight ahead at the altar, a beautiful, rounded wood with a blue marble border around it.

Then the crucifix caught his eye.

Patterson wasn't a Catholic, but he knew suffering when he saw it.

"Hey buddy," he said out loud. "I know just how you feel."

Father Norfill was turning the corner, coming from the sacristy, when he saw Patterson and walked up to him.

"Begging your pardon?" Father Norfill startled Patterson.

Patterson was too tired to jump. But he immediately turned to stare at the priest.

"Sorry, Bishop," Patterson said. "I didn't mean to disturb the peace."

"Mind if I sit down?" Father Norfill gestured to a seat two down in the row.

"Be my guest."

Father Norfill offered a silent prayer before continuing the conversation. "I take it you aren't a professed Catholic."

Patterson laughed "I'm not a professed anything. How did you know?"

It was Father Norfill's turn to chuckle. "Well, I'm not a bishop. And we don't get many visitors in here during the week."

"Your doors were open. I tried two other churches but they were locked."

"We have perpetual adoration," Father Norfill explained.

"What?"

Father Norfill pointed to the tabernacle off to the side. "We keep a host in the church, and it's open to come and pray at all times."

"Aren't you afraid of getting robbed?"

"Anyone who finds anything of monetary value to take is welcome to it," Father Norfill said. "We don't keep any money in the church anymore. And the chalice, ciborium, paten and communion cups are all locked up in the sacristy."

"I don't know what any of that stuff is," Patterson shrugged. "Anyway, I'm not the robber type."

"So, if you aren't here to rob us, then my guess is that Harrah's had something to do with your visit."

"Yeah," Patterson said, turning for the first time to get a good look at his conversational partner. "Lucky guess, eh, your holiness?"

Father Norfill laughed again. "I'm not the pope."

"What do they call you then?"

"Father. Sometimes Reverend. Although I discourage the latter reference."

"Well, Father sometimes Reverend. You've got a nice place here."

"I'd like to think so."

"Right away I felt something different coming in here. I haven't been to a church in a long time. Not since I was a kid actually."

"So, you grew up in the faith?"

"No, but whenever my single-mother moved us from one place to another, one step ahead of the landlord, she'd walk my brother and me to the nearest church, and pray that we wouldn't get caught."

"So, your mother prayed to God for protection then?"

"I have no idea. I never really asked her about it."

"But something must have rubbed off."

"How do you mean?" Patterson was slightly annoyed but he had been up for almost two days straight.

"Something caused you to come here this morning."

"Like you guessed. Harrah's."

Father Norfill looked at Patterson. "It really wasn't much of a guess. St. Rose is a small congregation and I know all the regular members."

"I asked the concierge to recommend a church and she said St. Rose," Patterson stifled a smile.

Father Norfill laughed again. "I think we have a soft spot there because of bingo."

"What about bingo?" Patterson asked.

"We host a bingo game every Friday night. It doesn't affect Harrah's proceeds much, but it's quite popular."

"Don't you think life is a lot like bingo?" Patterson asked. "We're forced to play the card we're given. And if that weren't bad enough, then you have to rely on someone else calling out the numbers to make anything of it."

Despite his bingo analogy, Patterson was methodical. Some of that trait had to do with his dad moving away when he was four.

Patterson had gotten an academic scholarship to Kalamazoo College. All of the moving around when he was young caused him to pay attention to details. This transferred over to the classroom, where he excelled. After getting a Bachelor's degree in engineering he was hired by Pharmacia which became Pfizer. He worked at their corporate headquarters in Kalamazoo for 23 years.

Being a production engineer and a top supervisor he was spared the series of layoffs that happened with each merger or take-over. But being financially secure didn't make up for an extreme lack of adventure.

Patterson never married. His early life presented the equation of:

family = mom – dad = major loss = instability.

Why sign up for unnecessary pain if you can avoid it, was his mantra. Despite the attempts of several female friends to run through his emotional obstacle course, none of them were successful. Bottom line: at mid-life, he was bored and had no significant other to talk him out of heading to Harrah's.

His house was almost paid for. His car was paid for. He was in great heath (chalk one up for good food choices and exercise). He read an average of three books a month. He wasn't a joiner but he had a few friends from work that he had supper with occasionally. But decades of predicable living had caught up with him.

So, here he was, on a very muggy Wednesday morning, sitting in St. Rose of Lima's having a conversation with a ministerial stranger.

"I don't think life is like bingo at all," Father Norfill answered, continuing their conversation.

"But it's so random. I mean, what are the odds that someone like me would travel 500 miles and then be here, having a conversation like this with a total stranger?"

"You're forgetting free will."

Patterson's laugh echoed across the empty church. "Sorry, but I don't believe in that. If I ever were to select a religion, I'd go with something that was very pre-deterministic."

Father Norfill raised his eyebrows, motioning for Patterson to continue.

"I mean, we don't select our parents. We don't choose where or when we're born. We're given our DNA unsolicited. Forgive me for saying this Father, but if there is a god, god is very much asleep at the wheel."

"But you decide what you do with all of that. Your upbringing, your environment, your DNA," Father Norfill countered "There are so many examples of extraordinary people who have overcome major obstacles."

"Sure. But they're extraordinary because they were the exception."

"I believe you are an exception as well," He looked right at Patterson.

"Why would you say that?"

"Rose of Lima, the patron saint of this church, was said to have been a pious person. She had a reverence for God. A devotion. A commitment. What are you committed to?"

Patterson was taken aback by this question. "I'm committed to my work."

Father Norfill shook his head. "What about God?"

"It's hard to be devoted to someone you don't know. Or understand. I'm no saint like Rose of Lima."

"She was a human being just like you and I. But she faced incredible pressure to conform. Choosing to ignore that pressure made her extraordinary. Just like you."

"Father, with all due respect, I came here to gamble. Let's keep that fact up front."

There was another smile coming across Father Norfill's face. "Then why did you ask the concierge at Harrah's to recommend a church?"

Patterson laughed. "My luck ran out. Pure and simple. I blew through two thousand dollars and have absolutely nothing to show for it."

As soon as the words came out of his mouth, Patterson had a flashback of when he was in junior high school. By this time his mother had been working for a women's Co-op. She eventually became an assistant manager, went back to college and earned a degree in Business Management. After completing her degree, the women's co-op chose her to be its next director. With the increase in salary, Patterson's mom was finally able to make a down payment on a home.

It was this economic godsend that spawned the Patterson family's newfound stability.

"Regardless of the stimulus, you still made a choice to come here," Father Norfill observed.

"Out of habit. That's all," Patterson replied. "In times of crisis, my mom fell back on what was familiar. And so did I."

Like the Sydnee McAllister incident when Patterson was a senior in college. They were in an English Lit class together. She sat right behind him. It began innocently enough. Sydnee was bright, outgoing and inquisitive. When Patterson ignored the taps on his shoulder, followed by the notes she passed him, Sydnee followed him out of class, across the quad, towards the Student Union.

"Hi," she began, smiling at him.

"Can I help you?" he asked, wondering why she couldn't take a hint.

"Would you like to study together for our mid-term?"

"I'm not much of a joiner."

She laughed. "Yeah. I've noticed that. Why don't we start a revolution over lunch?"

They sat their trays down in a corner table. Just enough out of the flow of things.

"I want to get out of this place with a 4.0 and get accepted to law school," she told him. "How about you?"

"Actually, I'm interested in knowing why after four years together in this place, you suddenly want to study together."

Sydnee shook her head. "It's not like that. I've been working overtime to get to know you. And time's running out. So, I figured, it's now or never."

"But, what's the point?"

"We still have four months left."

"It doesn't work that way with me." He felt himself getting embarrassed.

"It doesn't?"

"No, I'm not as extroverted as you are."

Sydnee whistled under her breath. "I'm not asking to date you. I'm just trying to get to know you."

"Relationships are complicated enough to begin with. Why invite disaster with a four-month timeline?"

"So that's why you've been ignoring my subtle invites?"

He smiled. "Partly."

"What's the other part?"

"Emotional intimacy takes time. You can't manufacture it," Patterson couldn't help eyeing the side exit that was conveniently close to them.

"Wow!" She whistled again. This time out loud. "Are you always this serious?"

"I've never been good at small talk."

"Sometimes small talk is a great way to get a real conversation going," She was adamant but empathetic.

"I understand the concept," he said. "But I'm not good at it, with women I mean."

"Everything doesn't have to be sexual."

"But, for me, relationships are linked to emotional intimacy." Now he was absolutely beet-red.

It was tough enough to have gone through a year of therapy just to find out why he was having major problems relating to people – especially to women. Now he was sitting face-to-face with someone of the opposite sex who seemed intent on getting to know him, no matter what.

Sydnee seemed undeterred. "Tell me your favorite color."

"That would be a toss-up between teal or turquoise."

"Now tell me a secret," She smiled. "Something you've never told anyone."

"I already did." He couldn't help smiling back.

"Yeah. I figured you aren't the type to go around bragging about the difficulty of intimate relationships."

She offered her hand up in the air for a high-five.

"Congratulations! You've just smashed your personal emotional sound-barrier!"

Patterson and Sydnee continued their conversation in the student lounge outside Sydnee's dorm that very same weekend. Over the course of the next four months, they became friends. As close as any that Patterson ever had.

But after graduation, Sydnee headed for Stanford and law school. Meanwhile, Patterson was offered a job at Pharmacia which eventually morphed into Pfizer.

Although the two of them exchanged letters during the first few months of school, the letters became less frequent. Then only greeting cards at the holidays.

Sydnee graduated from Stanford and worked in San Francisco for nearly two decades. Eventually she took a job at a law firm in Ann Arbor. Back in Michigan, Sydnee tracked down Patterson suggesting they get together when she was in Kalamazoo to visit her mother.

Neither one of them had been back to their alma mater since graduating. They agreed to lunch in Kalamazoo College's dining hall.

As they sat down at another corner table, Sydnee began the conversation. "So, how's life been treating you?"

"Work is good. I'm a production engineer at a pharmaceutical company. It's interesting work..."

She completed his sentence: "...and it doesn't involve too much personal interaction, right?"

"Well, if I weren't self-conscious before, I sure am now."

"I'm sorry. I really am," She looked straight at him. "But you can't lie to me. Remember? You've already opened up. In this very same place."

"But then you went to Stanford and fell off the face of the earth."

"I didn't fall off anything. I was in law school. In California. And I could just as easily have thought you fell off the face of the earth too!" She gently shoved him.

"You're really good at this lawyer thing," he said.

"So, the real question is, where do we go from here?"

He looked surprised. "You don't have a significant other?"

She showed him her hands that held no rings on them. "Nothing. Nada. I must have caught some of your chasteness."

He laughed.

She moved a little closer to him. "When was the last time you went on a date?"

"It's been a while."

"How long?"

He cleared his throat before answering. "Four years, maybe five."

Sydnee raised her eyebrows. "Please don't tell me the last woman you had a decent conversation with was me? Back here? Back in the day?"

"Yep."

"I rest my case," She stared him down. "Patterson, you are such a shmuck!"

"How can you remain so absolutely clueless?"

"About what?"

"Life!" She stood up. "I'm sorry, but I'm not going to stand by and watch you throw it away." And with that she turned around and walked out the door.

And that very conversation with Sydnee had more to do with Patterson sitting in St. Rose of Lima Church, next to Father Norfill, than anything else. Less than a month later, he was in Metropolis.

"But you already told me that you had very little experience with organized religion growing up," Father Norfill said, bringing Patterson back to the present.

Patterson nodded in the affirmative. "Keeping in mind that the little run-ins with God happened whenever mom was in a state of crisis. Somehow, she equated attending church with security. I don't."

"Then tell me, what exactly brought you to Metropolis?"

Patterson stretched his legs and gave a deep sigh before answering. "Father, I have a problem," he blurted out.

Father Norfill raised his eyebrows, signaling Patterson to continue.

"I don't take enough chances. Going to Harrah's was just a cover-up. It was nothing. I didn't actually risk anything of significance."

"How so?"

"I'm not sitting here, talking with you because I lost some money. I'm here because I'm disappointed."

"In organized religion?" Father Norfill offered his best guess.

"In myself. I don't trust myself enough to take emotional chances and it almost ruined the one relationship I have that matters to me."

"Which is?"

Patterson stood up. "Could I use your office for a moment?" he asked.

Father Norfill nodded his approval.

They walked through the church, out the side door that led to the rectory. Once inside, Father Norfill motioned toward the office.

"I need to make a phone call," Patterson explained.

"Tradition has it that St. Rose of Lima was a glutton for self-inflicted punishment. But she didn't need to inflict additional suffering on herself to be closer to Christ," Father Norfill said. "Jesus is more interested in relationship than religious rules." He smiled as he closed the office door behind him.

Patterson pulled out his cell phone and dialed Sydnee's number.

"I'm not sure that I should even be taking your call," she said.

"I need to tell you that you're absolutely right. Except for one small thing."

"Which is?"

"I'm more afraid than clueless, Sydnee. Especially with you."

"I'm your friend, Patterson. You should know that."

"And I want to be a good friend back."

"So, that's what has you stymied?"

"I don't know how to take the next step," he said. "And I don't want to screw it up. I've been talking with a priest."

"You went to confession?"

"I don't know what that is," he said.

"It's when you tell a priest your sins," she explained.

"I did, in a way. Toward the end of our conversation, I told Father Norfill that I don't take risks. And intimacy is a big emotional risk."

"It is for me too, Patterson. Why do you think I waited so long to get back in touch with you?"

"You were at Stanford."

"Yeah. And then I wasn't. But I still held off. I had stuff I needed to figure out. I'm an only child of only children. We didn't have big holiday get-togethers. My dad and mom were both professionals who didn't socialize a lot outside of work. And I didn't have a ton of people skills back in my college days. That day when we sat down in the cafeteria for the first time. I was winging it."

Patterson sighed. "Well, you did a great job, Sydnee."

"Thanks." She smiled at his compliment.

"It took a lot of guts for you to reach out the way you did," he said.

She smiled even wider. "Yeah. Well, having no social filter sometimes gets you into very unexpected places."

"Speaking of which, I'm calling you from Metropolis, Illinois."

Sydnee laughed. "The home of Superman?"

"Yeah."

"What are you doing there, Patterson?"

"Well, I thought I came here to gamble. There's a Harrah's casino, right along the Ohio River."

"I don't recall you being a gambler."

"I'm not. By a long shot."

Sydnee laughed. "You're using a gambling term to explain how much of a gambler you aren't."

"Please, stop being a lawyer for a second. I'm trying to open up."

"Patterson, that's a big step."

"I'm sorry for making excuses for so long," he swallowed hard, looking at the picture of St. Rose that was on the wall. "You're my best friend and I don't want to mess our friendship up."

"You haven't," she sighed. "When I walked away from you in the cafeteria, I realized I was walking away from myself. I didn't want to admit how much I care."

He was momentarily struck speechless as something deep inside him broke open.

"Sydnee. In this church office, there's a painting of St. Rose of Lima."

"OK"

"Father Norfill said she's famous for being beautiful but scorning suitors in favor of God."

"She must be the patron saint of everyone who goes dateless on Saturday night."

"I don't know about patron saints, but I think I understand her dilemma," Patterson said. "She thought she had to choose between having a boyfriend or God. But she could have had both. Actually, if you can't be emotionally intimate with a human being, I doubt you could be intimate with God."

Sydnee perked up. "The apostle John writes about that very thing in his gospel. He begins by saying God is love. He goes on to talk about how if we say we love God but hate our neighbor, we're a liar."

"I think you just hit the nail on the head!"

"I did?"

"Yeah." Patterson swallowed hard and continued, determined not to let fear get in the way this time. "Is this a good moment to ask you for a second date?"

"It is, Patterson," Sydnee sighed and smiled at the same time. "It is."

Evie McDonald and the Luck of the Irish

Evie was fidgeting when she checked into the Cardiology Department at Massac Memorial Hospital.

She was there to get a stress test. She was referred there because of the results of her most recent annual physical.

Great, she thought. *I'm only 34 and something's up with my blood pressure.*

Not that Evie was one to give in to worry. In fact, she was fierce in her determination to overcome that particular emotion. Not giving in to it had become her life's ambition.

That was after her mother and oldest brother (by 10 years), had passed away within two years of each other.

But before all this, there was her father.

At fourteen years of age Evie had emigrated from Northern Ireland with her own mother, Kathleen, whose husband had died from a car bombing in the Omagh City Center.

It was on August 15, 1998 that Tristen McDonald was with Kathleen and Evie, leisurely shopping on what looked to be a typical market day. Hundreds of townsfolk were gathered near each other looking for bargains as they chatted away.

A half-hour into their excursion Kathleen and Evie went to look at some fabrics, separating from Tristen as he wandered away from them. A few minutes later there was a buzz as local police, acting upon a tip, shooed folks away from an area with a suspected car bomb.

Unfortunately, the tip proved to be inaccurate and fatal. The police inadvertently moved the crowd directly into the path of most damage. In the end, 29 people were killed and 220 others were injured. The Real IRA claimed responsibility for the bombing. Meanwhile the RUC (Royal Ulster Constabulary) received blame for failing to act on prior warnings. And as late as 2017, no one had been convicted for the crime.

Tristen died from a concussion three days after being admitted to Omagh Hospital.

After the funeral mass, Kathleen decided that enough was enough. She had lived through the most recent version of The Troubles and was tired of it. She applied for a visa and received it. The generous settlement from Tristen's life insurance policy, combined with his work-related insurance, and vested pension allowed her to move to the United States.

Kathleen's nursing degree and additional schooling in Chicago eventually opened the door for her to apply for a job at Massac Memorial, where she had worked in the cardiology department.

The irony of the situation wasn't lost on her thirty-two-year-old daughter.

Kathleen had continued working until her chemotherapy treatments barely kept her on her feet. Then she decided to quit the chemo before the chemicals killed her.

"Mom," Evie had said with tears flowing. "This is your last hope!"

Kathleen laughed. "Honey, take a good look at me. Does this look hopeful?"

More tears.

"Come on, honey. I don't want your last memories of me to be of some fragile has-been. I want to leave this earth in one piece."

Evie's mom passed away in January.

In April, just as the daffodils were blooming and the forsythias were on the way, she received word about Martin.

Being the oldest in the family, and the only son, he decided to stick it out in Omagh after his father's untimely departure.

He had made up his mind before his father's funeral and had decided to drop the news during the wake.

"I'm not leaving," he told Evie.

"The rest of our family is moving to America. What's your alternative?"

"In case you haven't noticed, I've got a life here, Evie. A good job. A future."

"You're a Vauxhall salesman for crying out loud," she had protested. "What's so great about selling tiny cars that get good gas mileage?"

Martin was furious. "Top salesman six years running. I'd say you're a wee bit jealous because I knew what I wanted to do right out of university."

"Jealous?" Evie had shot back. "That you took a good education from Queen's University and flushed it down the loo?"

"Being all of fourteen, I suppose you have first-hand experience at that sort of thing," Martin answered. "I'm ignoring your cheekiness because you're too young to know better."

"I know enough to see someone who's foolhardy when I run into them!" Evie turned and walked away.

This wouldn't have been that terribly sad, under ordinary circumstances, but it was the last time she saw Martin alive.

Fast forward to the April after her mother's passing. A letter arrived in the mail, postmarked from Belfast. It was from a barrister. The short of it was that Martin had passed away. A delivery truck's tailgate had malfunctioned while dropping off new product, and Martin had been crushed by a brand-new Vauxhall Astra.

Evie went back to Omagh for the funeral, running into her long-ago playmate, Saoirse Walsh.

"Praise be!" Saoirse blurted out when she accidentally bumped into Evie. "If it isn't Evie McDonald in the flesh!" She paused a moment before going on. "I'm so sorry for your loss, Evie."

Evie had to take a good look at her before recognition kicked in. "Saoirse! I can't believe it. How long has it been?"

"Ages. At least since you and your mom left. I mean, after the bombing and all." Saoirse's eyes went large. "Oh, Evie! Look at me. Isn't it enough that you've got one tragedy to deal with, without me dredging up another?"

There wasn't a mean bone in Saoirse's body, but she did have a tendency towards speaking first and then thinking about it. At least in social situations.

Evie smiled. "That's ok. Truly. How have you been?"

"Would you believe I'm a barrister? Actually, it was our office that sent you the official notification of Martin's passing. What an awful way to go!"

"Pardon?"

"There's a reason why it's a closed casket situation," Saoirse said matter-of-factly. "The Vauxhall absolutely crushed his head. Like a pancake. Actually, his chest was sort of caved in too."

Evie paled at the details of her brother's demise.

Saoirse pressed on. "Anyway, I graduated from Queens University too. Just like Tristen. The law was actually my second choice."

"What was the first?"

Saoirse smiled. "You're going to laugh."

"No, I promise."

"I went into Queens determined to take a performing arts curriculum. I wanted to be a classical singer."

Evie raised her eyebrows. As far as she could recall, nothing in Saoirse's past would have pointed in that direction.

"But then I found out some practical information."

"Which was?"

"There aren't many Irish opera companies. It's just not a big thing over here. Especially in Northern Ireland."

"I'm sorry that it didn't work out."

"Oh no," Saoirse nudged her childhood friend. "It happened for the best. How about you?"

"I was a social worker," Evie began, offering no further details on that professional choice. "Then mom got sick and I sort of put that on hold. I moved in with her and started writing children's books in the hospital while she was receiving chemo."

"Wow! A published author!"

Evie nodded. "Do you remember the time we stood outside of the Catholic St. Patrick's Cathedral in Armagh and sang "Oh Danny Boy" at the top of our lungs? Then you insisted that we go over to the Protestant Church of Ireland's St. Pat's and do the same?"

"We were going to be God's answer to The Troubles, weren't we? But it's such a shame what happened to Martin. Your brother was so successful. He loved selling cars. It's just too bad one fell on top of him."

But Evie's friendship with Saoirse wasn't enough to lure her back to Ireland.

Perhaps it was because of the way that Evie was introduced to Metropolis in the first place.

Initially, Kathleen had moved with her daughter to Chicago, attracted to the city's deep Irish community. But she soon learned the difference between the Northern Irish and the Chicago brand. Plus, Chicago is roughly ten times the entire population of County Armagh. For Kathleen it was a bit too much.

As luck would have it, one day she was minding her own business, eating lunch in Northwestern Memorial Hospital's cafeteria. It was crowded so Kathleen took a seat next to a crew of operating room nurses. Among them was Maggie Holmes, who happened to be from Metropolis.

Very quickly Maggie and Kathleen began their own side-conversation, during which Maggie described a sleepy, riverboat town in southern Illinois, along the banks of the Ohio River.

"We get winters down there," Maggie explained. "But not like here. They're gentle. Like the people."

Over the course of that lunch, Maggie had unwittingly sold Kathleen on calling Massac Memorial Hospital's human resources department. She quickly found out there was an opening for an RN in their Cardiology Department. On a whim, Kathleen booked an interview. It went so well that she gave her two weeks' notice and sublet her apartment before packing up and moving to Metropolis with Evie.

Kathleen had been blessed with amazing instincts and her hunch about Metropolis proved to be correct. That is to say, she loved everything about the place. After her stint in the Windy City, she found Metropolis to be a breath of fresh air.

The icing on the cake was finding a small house on Catherine Street, within walking distance of downtown. Evie was resistant to the move at first. But then there was the Symons family – consisting of Willow and her daughter Delaney. The families lived next door to each other. Both were run by single mothers. Both had teenaged daughters who were about to enter their senior year of high school.

Their first meeting set the tone for their friendship.

Delaney was five feet-two inches, with blonde hair and riveting blue eyes. She was sitting on her front porch, enjoying the summer day. Evie was three inches taller with raven black hair and black eyes. She was walking toward Sixth Street.

"Downtown's the other way," Delaney said, in a warm, helpful tone.

Evie turned her head toward the voice. "How do you know I'm headed toward downtown?"

"Well, there isn't much of anything in the direction you're headed. Unless you want to go to the Dairy Queen."

Evie frowned at the reference.

"You're not from here, are you?"

"No. My mom and I were living in Chicago. Until she got a notion to move here."

Delaney laughed. "Welcome to Metropolis. The Dairy Queen is probably the only thing we've got that Chicago doesn't. Well, that and the Superman statue by City Hall. Have you seen it?"

Evie shook her head.

Delaney got up from the porch steps, walked over to Evie and took her by the arm. "We'll have to turn around and take a right on Fifth Street. It's only four blocks away."

By the time they were standing in front of Superman, Evie and Delaney were well on the way to becoming fast friends.

"Wow. That's quite a statue!" Evie whistled her appreciation.

Delaney laughed. "Yeah. It's twelve feet high and weighs two tons. Solid bronze. The first one was fiberglass and it didn't last too long."

"Why?"

"Vandals. Or curious people who wanted to see what Superman was really made of." Delaney pointed to the statue. "But he's not the biggest guy in town by a long shot."

"What do you mean?"

"When you and your mom came into town, didn't you notice Big Jim's?" (Delaney was referring to the statue of the same name, which sits prominently in front of a grocery store named for him. The grocery sets on East Fifth Street).

"Oh yeah! We pulled into the parking lot to get groceries because of him."

"That's how it begins with most people who aren't from here." Delaney summed up.

Throughout senior year, Evie and Delaney sat together during lunch. Evie proved to be the more introspective and quiet of the two. Delaney was the extrovert, proven to be the more outspoken. Both were opinionated, but Evie normally held hers until asked.

Even though they went to different colleges – University of Chicago for Evie; University of Illinois at Champaign Urbana for Delaney – they kept in touch and caught up with each other during breaks.

Evie earned a master's degree in social work, becoming a family counselor. Her parents had begun living separately a year before the Omagh bombing killed Tristen. For the sake of their children, the parents had agreed to go on family outings once a month.

It was Delaney who had married first. Ultimately choosing, Tim, a hometown guy who had lived two blocks away. Tim had gone to the University of Illinois as well, becoming a veterinarian and taking over a local practice in Metropolis.

After Evie graduated from the University of Chicago she stayed in the city, moving a few blocks off of Michigan Avenue when rents were still affordable. But when Kathleen's health began to decline, Evie made the move back to Metropolis to live with her, eventually becoming her caregiver.

As for marriage, there simply wasn't time for Evie to adequately explore that possibility. She had plenty of dates, at first. But her social work practice grew – to the point of striking out on her own. She was smart and empathetic and a fierce advocate for the mothers who were her clients.

Once Evie returned to Metropolis, it didn't take long for her and Delaney to pick up where they had left off years before.

By this time, Delaney was a freelance writer making a comfortable living working at home. She had majored in marketing in college, gotten a good internship, and excelled. Her genuine friendliness and ability to network paid off in spades. She and Tim had two children in grade school.

And now, Evie and Delaney were sitting in the Cardiology Department's waiting room.

"How are you doing?" Delaney asked, taking a good look at her friend, nudging her gently.

"Cut it out," Evie said, almost underneath her breath.

"I'm trying to redirect your sober-mindedness," Delaney said in her defense. "You're Irish. Aren't you supposed to be the one whose always in a frolicsome mood?"

"What?"

"What other country has leprechauns?"

Evie raised her eyebrows. "What other country has The Troubles?"

"Lots of countries have civil wars."

"And we're the grand ones for storytelling, right?"

Delaney smiled. "That's right! And I dare you to tell me a funny one right now."

"Here?" Evie glanced around the waiting room. "In Massac Memorial?"

"Why not?"

"Because I'm thinking you'll start to laugh, like a hyena, and the rest of the patients here will get infected and we'll get kicked out."

"You're stalling, Evie. Get on with it!"

Evie took a good look at her friend before answering. "Choose your setting first. Ireland or here?"

"Ireland." Delaney said without skipping a beat. "It's more romantic."

"There was the time when I was a little girl. Mom had taken off her slip to iron it. She was starting to put it back on when, all of a sudden, dad comes downstairs into the living room and starts feeling a little randy."

"Randy?"

"As in, physically excited."

"Oh."

"And he takes one look at mom and starts to make a move toward her. So, mom steps into the kitchen and he chases her back and forth. He's not even noticing that I'm in the room. Mom says to him, 'Tristen, if you know what's good for you, you'd better stop.' To which he replies, 'But I do know what's good for me.' Mom puts up her hand and points to me and says, 'Your daughter is watching!' Dad takes a good look and says, 'Well, she's got to learn sometime.' And he starts to laugh so hard the he slips and falls down."

"Classic!" Delaney said, stifling a laugh. "Now, don't you feel better?"

"Not especially."

Delaney nudged her friend again. "Come on, admit it."

A smile slowly started to work its way across Evie's face.

Delaney broke into a grin and, trying to stifle another laugh, snorted.

"You sound like a prize piglet," Evie said. "Aren't you proud of yourself?"

"I am!"

Evie put her hand on Delaney's. "Do you remember the time we accidentally tripped the fire alarm in the cafeteria? It was the only time I wound up in the high school principal's office."

"It wasn't an accident."

"What?"

"I pulled it because the lunch lady had the audacity to serve us goulash that day." Delaney explained. "You just happened to be standing by me."

"An innocent bystander. After all these years, I find out that I was framed."

"Well, you could have come clean and exonerated yourself to the lunch lady before she called the principal."

Evie tightened her grip on Delaney's hand. "Our friendship has never worked that way."

Delaney looked at her friend and fought back a tear. "I know."

"Tell me another story."

"Ireland or here?"

"Make it a Metropolis story!" Delaney was now grinning from ear-to-ear.

"Remember the first walk we took?"

"To see the Superman Statue?"

Evie nodded. "Well, once we got to Superman Square, and checked him out, you mentioned kryptonite. I thought the whole thing was idiotic. That somehow, my mom had been tricked into moving to a city where they openly worshipped oversized men." She paused for effect, "Remember you told me about Big Jim?"

Delaney nodded her head.

"For a solid week after that, I kept walking around town looking for other monuments. Everywhere mom and I went. I was on the lookout. I swear, if she had come home one day after work and told me there was a statue of some other big guy in town, I would have called one of my friends in Chicago, packed my bags and taken the next bus out of town."

"No kidding?"

"Luckily for me, high school started soon and things started to look more normal."

"Until I told you that the Birdman of Alcatraz was buried here?"

Evie laughed. "Yeah. I almost forgot about that one!"

"So, how are you doing?"

"About looking for superheroes?"

"About dealing with life. With stress."

Evie sighed as the RN from cardiology came into the waiting room, calling out her name.

"Better," she said, giving Delaney a hug.

The Gazebo

Amy Theron sat on the steps of the gazebo in Washington Park. It was early May. A beautiful day. Sitting there, she savored her peanut butter and strawberry jam sandwich. An apple would provide a fresh dessert.

She worked at the Metropolis Public Library as one of the program assistants, focused on special events. She was thinking about one of them when a voice interrupted her.

"Amy?"

She looked up to see Mason Whittaker walking toward her.

"Mason? Goodness, talk about a blast from the past!"

They had come very close to dating during senior year in high school twenty years ago. But graduation had gotten in the way.

Then college and, for Mason, moving away from southern Illinois.

"Mind if I join you?"

She nodded, patting the space next to her.

"What brings you to our part of the world?" she asked.

"I'm interviewing for an air traffic controller position at Barkley Regional Airport. After fifteen years at Chicago O'Hare, I'm ready for something a little less demanding."

Mason had attended Purdue University and obtained a degree in air traffic control. From the time he was a little boy, he was fascinated with airplanes. Since first grade he worked to save money for a pilot's license and earned it when he was a senior in high school. His grandfather had told him stories about barnstormers that came to Metropolis to the fairgrounds just outside of town. They entranced crowds of farmers who came to watch them perform.

Although Mason was an adventurous person by nature, he was also shy when it came to matters of the heart, including dating.

After four years of admiring Amy from afar, he had almost summoned up the courage to ask her out a few days before graduation. Each time he saw her in the cafeteria, in the hallway, waiting for the bus, Amy was with other friends and that was enough to stop him.

"I'm no world traveler, but O'Hare has got to be one of the busiest airports in the world," she said.

Amy was simply telling the truth, clearly impressed with her friend's work history. On the other hand, she easily coordinated lots of interesting events, bringing the world to Metropolis, without thinking of it with any self-importance.

"Close to sixty air traffic controllers working from four different towers," Mason confirmed, as he eagerly switched subjects, preferring to find out more about Amy. "And by the looks of it, I'd guess that you work close to this gazebo."

"I do," she answered, as she pointed across the street to the library.

"You were always answering questions in class," he remembered. "And you were on so many committees."

While Mason spent after-school time concentrating on sports, Amy had been busy with debate, drama, and future teachers club.

Sitting next to Amy, he began to feel himself tripping over his words. He thought, *Why do my emotions keep getting in the way of having a decent conversation with a potential date? I might as well be back in high school, stammering my way toward not asking Amy out.*

Of course, Amy had no problem continuing the conversation. She grew up with two older brothers. Her siblings were kind, thoughtful, and included their sister in pick-up games of basketball, baseball or most any other neighborhood sport. She developed into a very athletic person, but once in high school, chose not to continue in that direction.

"How does it feel, coming back to the old home town?" Amy looked at Mason and smiled.

"Chicago is big, but it's still the Midwest," he began. "I've really never left this part of the country."

As soon as he moved to the Windy City, Mason had loved it. Grant Park, the Museum of Science and Industry, the Art Institute, the National Museum of Mexican Art, and others. He settled in the Avondale neighborhood - a very easy commute to work.

He especially appreciated getting to and from work via the Chicago Transit Authority (CTA) and because O'Hare was in the opposite direction of downtown, he mostly avoided the crowds of neighbors who headed into the city for work.

On weekends, when he explored the city, it was a snap. And he discovered that he loved the Hispanic culture prevalent among his neighbors, having a mom who shared that heritage.

Growing up, it hadn't been easy for Mason. Being mixed-race in a small town was fraught with challenging circumstances. In elementary school, students who stood out were likely to be targeted or misunderstood by their peers. In high school, the fact that he was an excellent athlete helped him gain acceptance.

It also helped that Mason's dad and mom shared a view of life that celebrated cultural differences. Their example taught him to view diversity as a strength. Francisca, his mom, was an elementary school teacher. Warren, his father, was a lawyer, who worked for the Legal Aid Society. They had met when Warren was in college serving an internship with a non-profit agency and Francisca was working a summer job as a community organizer at the same agency.

After college, the two were offered jobs in Massac County. They weren't Metropolis natives, but they were extremely committed to the city and the people who lived there.

Amy's parents were more traditional. Both had recently retired from working for the city.

Amy grew up being comfortable with who she was, and it was reflected in her easygoing approach to life. In college, her choice of graduate study reflected her curiosity. She loved helping others access factual information that helped broaden their point of view.

So, although she was raised as what a pollster might label a "conservative," she was anything but. Her own experience taught her that life is full of interesting options and she loved exploring them.

"I remember you as being a quiet thinker," Amy said, looking right at Mason. "Especially in social ethics class our senior year."

The memory came back quickly to Mason. "That was my favorite class! Not so much for the discussions, although some of them were great. But I learned to listen before speaking. Miss Rehmer was great about reinforcing how we needed to slow down and quit formulating responses in defense of our own position."

Amy nodded. "She was absolutely my favorite teacher in high school. Before taking her class, I was always concentrating on defending my position. I mean three years of debate club would do that to anyone. Miss Rehmer taught me the art of conversation."

Mason smiled. "Yeah. My mom was a great one for joining any social cause. I guess it was in her DNA. She thought Dolores Huerta was a saint."

"Dolores helped found the United Farm Workers, right? With Cesar Chavez?"

Mason nodded. "As it turned out, she was more consistent in her treatment of others than Cesar was. My mom used Dolores as an example of how to take care of people around you. Actually, both my parents were great. I moved to Avondale because of them."

"What do you mean?"

"I wasn't your typical Chicago resident," he explained. "I didn't hang out downtown. I spent more time being involved in my own Avondale neighborhood. A lot of Hispanic families helped each other. I loved it. That's probably what I'm going to miss most if I get the job here." Again, he switched the subject. "But what about you? Why did you stay in Metropolis?"

Amy took a deep breath. "My dad and mom were natives and worked for the city. But after high school I went to the University of Illinois at Urbana-Champaign. Majored in English Lit."

"So, who's your favorite writer?"

"Jane Austen."

He nodded. "She's toward the top of the list for me too!"

She thought, *Anyone who likes Jane Austen is worth keeping as a friend! I wonder why we didn't connect in high school? I would have gone out with Mason if he'd only asked me!*

"After college there was an opening at the Metropolis Public Library for a circulation and programming assistant. It didn't require a library science degree and they hired me."

"And you've been here ever since?"

Amy smiled. "Yeah. I'm really a small-town girl at heart. I love being part of the community. When people come to our library it's a sign that they're curious. That's exciting. And don't get me started on the young readers programs we have."

Because this conversation was taking place during the lunch hour, Amy had to excuse herself. "See you later," she called as she headed back to work.

About a week later, she was grocery shopping at Big Jim's, walking along the produce aisle, absorbed with the greens section. Once again, she was pleasantly distracted when she heard Mason's voice.

"Hey! What are the chances?" he said, grinning.

"A person has to eat, right?" She laughed.

"You were really checking out the lettuce," Mason said, "Like you were contemplating it."

"Actually, I was thinking about the workers who picked it."

"My mom had us say a prayer for the hands that harvested the food we ate," he said. "It became such a habit that I still do it."

Because they both had other engagements after shopping the conversation was a short one.

A week later they ran into each other again at Big Jim's.

"I got the air traffic controller job!" he announced, with a big grin. "I'm living with my parents here in town, for the time being."

"Do you think you'll be staying in Metropolis?" she asked, not trying to hide the fact that she wished he would.

"My parents are looking to move out west. I might buy their house."

Amy smiled before continuing the conversation. "Why don't you come over for dinner sometime?"

She noticed that Mason didn't wearing a wedding ring. Neither did she.

That Saturday they sat down together to a meal of roast chicken, mashed potatoes, fresh green beans, and salad.

"This is absolutely delicious!" Mason was at his best during a meal. The food seemed to be a natural way to invite conversation. A glass of wine helped loosen his tongue.

"Isn't it a little perplexing how life turns out sometimes?" he began. "We went to the same high school. I often wanted to strike up a conversation with you. But it always seemed like you were surrounded by friends."

Amy leaned forward. "There are all kinds of friends," she said. "Mostly they were friends because of the clubs we were part of. It wasn't until college that I formed stronger relationships."

"I really miss Avondale," he confessed, speaking of his former neighborhood in Chicago. "We were a group of families that cared about each other."

"It must have been hard to grow up here - a place that isn't as diverse as Chicago."

Mason was reluctant to talk about himself. "mom and dad were into helping people. They attended the University of Chicago because they were smart and got scholarships. They met while interning for a non-profit together. Plus, they had strong faith."

"But what about you?" Amy asked.

"I pretty much followed their lead," Mason answered. "For them, Jesus was all about looking out for the underdog. He was an underdog himself."

"And a witness to the power of love." Amy wasn't exactly a religious person, in the sense of regular church attendance. Her parents had encouraged her to believe that everyone had a soul, and to treat everyone with kindness. But she didn't have a lot of experience with organized faith.

"My mom's Catholic," he said. "She really believes in the social gospel. She grew up right after the church instituted Vatican II. It was a time of focusing on social issues. Mom saw Jesus reflected in people who didn't have a whole lot. My dad was the same. It was a really solid foundation."

Amy took a bite of food before continuing. "My parents grew up here. They worked for the city and were very practical people."

True statements, but they barely scratched the surface.

Amy's family had enough to pay the bills but they didn't have a lot left over for frivolous spending. What money they saved often went to help others. Amy's dad was a carpenter with the city's public works department. Her mom was a bookkeeper for the utilities department.

"My parents volunteered at a neighborhood food pantry," Amy said. "They helped coordinate holiday distributions. It was a real eye-opener for me to see all the families who needed help."

Mason nodded. "My parents volunteered with Habitat for Humanity in Paducah. Having a home was really important to them. They rented out a couple of homes here in town and spent a lot of time working with their renters to develop stronger life skills."

"Did you save room for some homemade dessert?" She had made brownies that day.

Mason smiled. "If it's half as good as the main meal, I'm hoping that you'll offer a take-home bag!"

Amy's laugh came from a deep place of feeling comfortable in her own shoes, and in her own house. It wasn't fancy, but everything about it bore her stamp. While she excused herself to get the dessert, Mason examined the photographs in the dining room.

There were pictures of Amy's family, mostly outside, almost always smiling. The love they shared with each other was perfectly evident. Mason noticed that none of the photos were posed or appeared to be taken by a professional.

He also spotted a photo of a couple taken a few generations back. It was a picture of a farming family in a field. The father was dressed in overalls and boots, the mother sitting near him, with three children sitting beside them.

Amy returned with the brownies.

"I bet there's a story behind the photo of this family."

"It's my dad's family," Amy explained "My grandpa was a farmer, near Round Knob. He had eighty acres, mostly in corn. My dad is the youngest in the picture, with his two older sisters."

Mason took another look. "Your dad is the only one of the kids who's looking directly at the camera. And he looks like he's about to tell a joke.'

Amy smiled. "He's got a great sense of humor. It helped me a lot growing up. I could get away with just about anything, if I could make him laugh about it."

"For instance?"

"Once dad and I were at the library. I had an overdue book with a fine on it. I told dad I didn't have to pay the fine because I was related to Lois Lane."

Mason burst out laughing at the reference to Clark Kent's (AKA Superman's) girlfriend.

"See how it works?" she smiled.

"Did you still have to pay the fine?"

Amy nodded. "And to think, now I work there!"

"Which is more important to you? Having a sense of humor or having faith?" Mason's question was heartfelt.

"It depends upon how you look at faith," she began. "Webster's primary definition of faith is strong belief or trust in someone or something. The secondary definition is belief in the existence of God. For me, the first definition is much more important that the second."

"Why is that?"

"It's pretty hard to have faith if you don't have trust. Thomas is my favorite apostle. He wasn't afraid to admit he had doubts. Even after following Jesus for three years. I don't go to church much but I've read the Bible. It's one of my favorite books."

"Thomas wasn't afraid to say that he didn't understand," Mason agreed. "He spoke up during the Last Supper and asked Jesus 'We don't know where you are going, so how can we know the way?'"

"Wonder is a big part of growing faith. So much of growing in a relationship, of developing trust, has to do with being open to being awestruck."

Mason munched on a brownie while getting back to his question. "So, which is more important to you, humor or faith?"

Amy leaned towards her dinner guest. "Does it have to be an either/or choice? Faith or humor? Especially if you're talking about faith in something as big as God; couldn't God be big enough to intertwine them both?"

"You're saying that God is bigger than what we think?"

Amy smiled. "Much bigger." She leaned back and opened up her arms really wide. "I caught a fish this big, but it keeps on getting bigger!"

At this revelation Mason laughed. "This is, by far, the best conversation I've had in years," he said. "Not to mention your cooking!"

"No problem," Amy grinned. "Next time you can host the meal."

Acknowledgments

I'd like to thank:

My family (Mom, Dad, Douglas, Dianna, David, Dorothy, Dominic, Donna and Deborah);

Roger Heldt (friends since grade school, and one of the most creative people I know), for the amazing cover art;

Marjorie Turner Hollman (developmental editor) and Anne Parker (copyeditor and book design) – this book bears the fruits of their efforts!

Russ Eanes, who offered wisdom, expertise and guidance along the path to publication.

Rosemary Baxter, Director of the Metropolis Public Library, for her interest in the book, and for taking the picture of the gazebo in Washington Park, which is part of the quilt on the book's front cover.

An extremely heart-felt thank you to the town of Metropolis, and small towns everywhere!

And thanks to God, from Whom all gifts flow...